喚醒你的英文語感！

Get a Feel for English !

【推薦序一】

英文多一點　健身 High 一點

　　談「健身英文」，問我就對了！從前的我，就像大多數的台灣學生一樣，只把英文當成需要死背的考試科目，而不是自然的溝通應對工具；但在進入健身中心工作後，我赫然發現，無論是為了進修或教學，英文都是不可或缺的基本能力！我必須用英文學習來自紐西蘭的新課程，也得在課堂上使用大量的英文術語指導台下的學員，更別說幾乎所有的參考資料和相關書籍都是國外的「原汁原味」進口版，再加上有時「PT 個人教練指導課程」面對的就是金髮碧眼的洋人，只有硬著頭皮上場；結果，原本不太敢開口說英文的我，現在不但每天說，而且還愈說愈起勁。

　　對專業老師來說，休閒產業的國際化已是大勢所趨，英文聽說讀寫的能力當然成為「必要的」工具；對健身迷來說，了解相關專有名詞及簡單的英文會話，能讓你連出國時都能到健身房快樂地運動，無論是器材的使用或是與教練的溝通，都會更加輕鬆順暢。

　　或許有些人會認為出國到健身房的機會畢竟不多，再者，「肢體語言」本身就是國際語言，透過模擬老師的動作，人人都可跟著作，難道英文真的有那麼重要？事實上，這可是關鍵所在！這些年來我深切體會到「英文多一點，健身 high 一點」，若是學員能聽得懂基本的英文術語並且了解多一些相關詞彙，不但能提升運動表現，且在目前講求流暢性且系統化的課程編排趨勢下（台灣各大健身房之 Body Combat, Body Pump, Body Balance, Body Jam 等課程都是由國際機構統一編排），懂英文就能跟得上課程節奏，並經由老師的提示知道下一步要做什麼，而不至於手忙腳亂，進而提升運動效率。

　　我的著作《塑型健身 72 變》是針對想改變自己的人所寫的健身入門書，而這本《健身英文很有聊》，我認為倒可以將它視為健身的進階書。因為市面上的英語學習書，大多只是把健身或運動相關的辭彙和基本會話放在其中的一兩個章節，還沒有像這本書如此完整的收錄編製成一冊，除了傳達身心靈健康和營養飲食的全方位健康概念外，更兼顧在健身房「隨時隨地練英文」的功效，相信讀完本書後，遇到老外來搭訕哈啦，也會變得「很有聊」！

亞力山大休閒健身俱樂部專任有氧老師　余明權

【推薦序二】
健康是永遠不退的流行

在這個天涯若彼鄰的地球村，英文早已是現代人基本的語言能力，健康更是人類永恆的生存基礎。運動健身的風潮在歐美相當盛行，並且經常發展出各種新式運動。近幾年來東方講究深層調息、平衡內在的練習法更是風靡全球。因此，對我這個熱愛健康養生的運動者來說，英語能力不但幫助我進修，跟上最新的運動潮流，對於推廣健康運動也息息相關。

舉例來說，台灣練瑜伽（Yoga）的人口快速增加，這項健身運動來自印度古老的養生智慧，能柔軟肢體、調節體質。另一項也講究肢體、呼吸的運動是彼拉提斯（Pilates），這項運動來自德國的醫療運動科學，能穩定核心肌群。現在更有瑜伽提斯運動（Yogalates）結合兩者的菁華，融合東西方的健康養生智慧。可見運動也有全球化的趨勢呢！

回想起我在美國攻讀研究所的時期，英文能力就是我不斷努力的一環。無論是上課或研讀各類資料文獻，語言都是一個必備的工具。在我開始專攻瑜伽提斯時，也同時進修語言，讓我沒有隔閡地收集正確的第一手資訊。遇到不同國家的健康運動同好，大家會分享彼此的養生經驗及健康新資訊，這時英文就是我們溝通的橋樑。我們會探討身體結構、生理學、人體工學、肌動學、復健醫療、身心學，研究瑜伽的八支功法和體位法，其中許多細微精緻的養生健康奧妙，都能激盪出令我們嘆微觀止的喜悅。

在《健身英文很有聊》我也看到了這樣的心意和樂趣。這本書的英文書名是「Healthy Living」，也就是「健康生活」，包含「健身」、「修心」、「飲食」三個主題。內容豐富又輕鬆有趣，不僅可使大家得到健康，更同時增進語言能力。而且，它是一本關於健康的會話書，目的是要幫助讀者與人交流溝通的。記得當初也是因為強力瑜伽的研習課程，才認識了貝塔出版社愛好健康運動的英文編輯 Mark。

以健康會友真是一件開心的事。最近我的第二本書《瑜珈提斯深呼吸》即將出版，風潮唱片也將發行我的瑜珈提斯 DVD，並很榮幸應貝塔出版社之邀請受訪，讓我能與更多人分享健康生活的心得。健康是現代人共通的話題，也是永遠不退的流行，永遠值得追求的時尚。相信《健身英文很有聊》也能帶給各位熱愛健康生活的好朋友，更多美好與快樂！

祝　　好書暢銷、長紅！

美國運動管理碩士　台灣首位瑜珈提斯專家　唐幼馨 Tina

【推薦序三】

走進世界　迎向健康

　　我會踏上整體醫療這條路，歷經人生中的幾個轉捩點，而且和英文有關。1997 年，我為了父親的癌症遠赴歐洲取「經」，在英國第一次看到 Naturopathy 這個字。這個字是由「nature」（自然）加上字尾「-pathy」（療法）組成，也就是「自然療法」的意思。自然療法主張病人有與生俱來的自癒潛力，醫生若能從各方面激活這種能力，病人就能恢復健康。深入瞭解這門醫學後，我內心激起一種莫名的悸動。我領悟到：醫生須不斷思考、精進、學習，尋求各種療法，使病人得到最人性化的照顧和治療。

　　之後，於 1997 年至 2001 年間，我遊歷歐洲各國學習各種自然療法。在奧地利，我學習草本醫學和旅館醫院預防醫學的經營；在德國，我學到自由基醫學、順勢醫學、高熱療法、能量醫學、生物療法和針灸水針療法等；在英國，我認識了花精情緒療法和舞蹈視覺音樂療法等概念；在瑞典，我學習順勢藥品的製作；在瑞士，我學習強調回歸自然的人智醫學。

　　有人或許認為這些是非正統的另類療法，但我深深感覺其科學性、成熟性和未來性，皆可彌補我國醫療環境之不足。有鑑於此，我在 2002 年決定走出傳統醫學的框架，邁向整合自然和現代醫學之路，並且在臺灣臺北成立了東西整合醫學中心，結合各式各樣的自然療法，應用在各種疑難雜症上。目前，中心的病人來自於臺灣全國各地，還有自香港、菲律賓、日本、加拿大、美國、比利時和安曼等地遠道而來的。

　　2003 年我赴德國開會，在飛機上的一本雜誌上讀到有關 Holistic Medicine（整體醫學）的文章，再次讓我激動不已。我發現自己欠缺診斷病人心靈癥結的技術，以至於無法發揮整體醫學的療癒功效。經過整整兩年的時間，我從能量醫學成功地發展出一套情緒診斷治療的方法，終於能進一步掌握身、心、靈整體診斷和治療的精髓。

　　2005 年年底，我的《整體醫學》第二冊即將出版，臺灣國際自然醫學院也正在籌設中，希望將東西結合的自然醫學傳承和進一步發揚。此外也正與其它健康事業商談異業結盟的可能性，希望臺灣成為健康輸出大國。

　　語言多麼奇妙啊！因為對幾個英文單字的好奇心，就改變了我身為一位醫生的態度和使命，也讓我的生命更加豐富。英文不但帶我走入世界，也把世界帶來給我。《健身英文很有聊》包含「身體」、「心靈」、「飲食」這三個健康生活的基本主題，內容輕鬆活潑、淺顯易讀，不但能學習英文，還能學到實用的健康知識。誠摯地希望本書能成為您走進世界、迎向健康的入門磚！

東西整合醫學中心　院長　　何逸僊醫師

◼ Diane Wei 黛安・衛

 CDI-02

This little firecracker never stops mov'in and shak'in and lives by the catchphrase, "Actions speak louder than words." Diane is always ready for a new adventure. She has always been interested in leading a well-rounded lifestyle, which becomes even better when she adds exercise to it. Get ready to get fit because hanging out with this dynamite girl is surly to inspire great things.

像小爆竹似的黛安總是活蹦亂跳、閒不下來，而她生活的口號就是「坐而言不如起而行」。黛安隨時準備好展開一段全新的冒險。她一直興致沖沖地過著充實的生活，加入運動後更是多采多姿。準備好迎向健康吧，因為和這個超ㄅㄧㄤˋ的可人兒在一起，保證好事連連喔！

◼ Alan Li 艾倫・李

Alan is a journalist for the Arts and Living section of a local newspaper. He is always busy with friends, work and hobbies. Recently Diane sparked a new interest in Alan, which developed into a new hobby of going to the gym. Being a journalist he is naturally drawn to the facts and digging up information is exactly what Alan does to embrace this new lifestyle.

◼ Jerry Mok 傑瑞・莫

If Diane's motto is "fit for life" than Jerry's is "sit for life." He spends his days on the couch, with the remote control in one hand and a beer in the other. Some might say Jerry isn't motivated, but actually he is. You can always rely on him for game times! Going the extra mile for a beautiful lady is never a problem to him. And like any great friend, he is always the

艾倫是一家地方報社的生活藝文版記者。他總是為朋友、工作和嗜好忙碌。最近黛安激發了艾倫的一項新興趣，讓他逐漸養成了健身房的新嗜好。身為記者，艾倫自然會被事實真相所吸引，而挖掘資訊也讓他欣然接受這種新的生活方式。

first to go to the store if the beer supply is low.

如果黛安的座右銘是「健康生活」，那麼傑瑞的就是「坐著賴活」。他終日耗在沙發上，一手握遙控器，一手拿啤酒。有人可能會說傑瑞不夠積極，但實際上正好相反。玩樂時，靠他準沒錯！為了美女奔波勞苦，對他而言絕不成問題。而且，就像任何上道的好朋友一樣，如果啤酒不夠了，他總是跑第一個去商店的人。

目　錄

CONTENTS

Preface 推薦序

Character Profile 人物介紹

Section One: Body Talk 強健體魄

Section Two: Shaping the Soul 休養性靈

Section Three: You Are What You Eat 均衡飲食

Interview 專題訪談

Section One

Body Talk 強健體魄

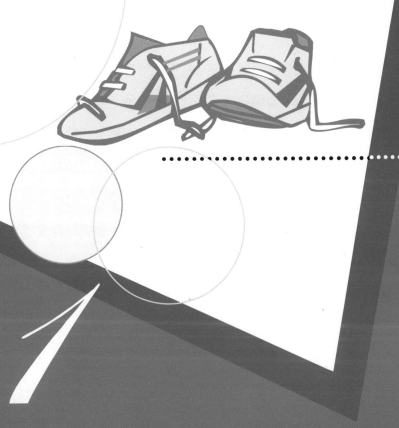

Chapter 1

Finding Fitness
健美路上你和我

怕你還沒聽說——電視迷落伍啦，健身迷才上道。上健身房不再是那些只練「身材」不練身體的肌肉猛男和健美靚女的專利。沒錯，以前亮出健身中心會員卡就聽到一句：「哇塞，你有上健身房喔？」的日子已經過去。健身中心已提升到一個新的層次。如今，喜歡健身成了生活的準則。

 CDI-03

In case you haven't heard, couch potatoes are out and fitness buffs are in. Going to a gym is no longer about beefy guys and perfectly polished women working "it" instead of working out. No, those days of flashing a gym pass and getting an "Oh wow, you go to the gym?" have passed. Fitness centers have moved up to a new level. It is now the norm to be fitness-friendly.

基本行話　　The Lingo

CDI-04

❶ fitness center [ˈfɪtnɪs ˌsɛntɚ]	健身中心 *n.*
❷ muscle [ˈmʌsl̩]	肌肉 *n.*
❸ workout [ˈwɝkˌaʊt]	運動；鍛練 *n.*
❹ exercise [ˈɛksɚˌsaɪz]	運動；訓練 *n.*
❺ access [ˈɛksɛs]	門路；取得的方法、權利 *n.*
❻ personal trainer [ˈpɝsn̩l̩ ˈtrenɚ]	私人教練 *n.*
❼ facility [fəˈsɪlətɪ]	設備 *n.*
❽ membership fee [ˈmɛmbɚʃɪp ˌfi]	會員費 *n.*
❾ locker [ˈlɑkɚ]	置物櫃 *n.*
❿ changing room [ˈtʃendʒɪŋ ˌrum]	更衣室 *n.*

暖身練習 Word Workout

CDI-05

A: I want to join a gym. Do you know of any good ones?
B: Sure. You can check out my **fitness center**. It's great!

A: 我想加入健身房。你知道有哪幾家不錯嗎？
B: 當然。你可以到我去的健身中心看看。很棒喔！

A: My goal is to build **muscle** mass. What kind of **workout** should I do?
B: Your trainer can help you design an **exercise** program that fits your needs.

A: 我的目標是練出一身肌肉。我該做什麼樣的鍛鍊呢？
B: 你的教練會設計一套符合您需求的健身計劃表。

A: As a member you have **access** to a **personal trainer**.
B: That's great. Do I also have full use of all of the **facilities**?

A: 身為會員，您有權找一位私人教練。
B: 太好了。我也可以任意使用全部的設備嗎？

A: When you pay your **membership fee** I will give you the key to your **locker**.
B: Great. Are there towels in the **changing rooms**?

A: 您繳清會員費時，我就會將置物櫃的鑰匙交給您。
B: 好極了。更衣室裡有毛巾嗎？

健美會話1　　　　Talk the Talk

CDI-06

(Alan and Diane are on the phone.)

Diane: I'm going to the gym today.

Alan: You said that last week and again two days ago. I haven't seen any sweat yet!

Diane: Hey, you have to look the part to play the part. I spent those days getting an exercise-**friendly** haircut and the right **outfit**.

Alan: Are you sure you're not just hesitating because you are **intimidated**?

Diane: Of what? **Slim** women and **buff** men don't scare me. Anyway, I don't see you jumping onto the **fitness** train with me.

Alan: Are you suggesting I go to the gym? Not a chance. Those **exercise machines** are impossible to figure out and the loud music gives me a headache.

Diane: Come on. We can be workout buddies. And the gym has a special **promotion** this month-seven days **free trial** and a discount if you **sign up** with a friend.

Alan: OK. I'll take a look, but I'm not promising anything!

Diane: Great! I'll pick you up in 30.

（艾倫和黛安正在講電話）

黛安：我今天要上健身房。

艾倫：妳上禮拜就說過了，兩天前也才說過一次。我連一滴汗都還沒看到！

黛安：嘿，扮什麼就要像什麼。我過去幾天忙著剪適合運動的髮型，買恰當的行頭。

艾倫：妳確定妳不是因為被嚇到怕了所以遲遲不肯行動嗎？

黛安：怕什麼？窈窕女和肌肉男嚇不了我的。不管怎樣，我看你是不會和我一起投入健身行列的。

艾倫：妳是在暗示我也該上健身房嗎？門兒都沒有。誰搞得清楚那些運動器材要怎麼怎麼操作，而且那震耳欲聾的音樂讓我頭痛。

黛安：來嘛，我們可以成為運動搭檔。而且那家健身房這個月有特別促銷活動──免費試用七天，如果和朋友一起報名還有折扣呢。

艾倫：好吧，我會去看看，但我不做任何保證喔！

黛安：太棒了！我三十分鐘內去接你。

 Words & Phrases

1. -friendly *suf.* 與名詞連用構成形容詞，表示「對……有幫助或無害的」

2. outfit [ˋaʊtˏfɪt] *n.* 裝備；服裝

3. intimidate [ɪnˋtɪməˏdet] *v.* 威嚇；脅迫

4. slim [slɪm] *adj.* 苗條的；纖弱的

5. buff [bʌf] *adj.* 強壯有肌肉的

6. fitness [ˋfɪtnɪs] *n.* 身體健康

7. exercise machine [ˋɛksəˏsaɪz məˏʃɪn] *n.* 運動器材

8. promotion [prəˋmoʃən] *n.* 促銷

9. free trial [ˋfi ˋtraɪəl] *n.* 免費試用

10. sign up 報名參加

 健美會話2 Walk the Walk

CDI-07

(At the gym)

Alan: I told you so about the music. You can hear it all the way down the street.

Diane: It's to get you **pumped** so you have energy to use all of these facilities. Hey, there's the front desk. Oh, and look at the **hunky** guy standing behind it!

Hank: Hi. Welcome to Body World. I'm Hank.

Diane: Uh...hi! We want to sign up for a one-year membership.

Alan: No, you do. I'm just here for ...

(A beautiful woman walks up to Alan)

Stella: Hi, I'm Stella. I'm a personal trainer here. I can help you with all of your training needs.

Diane: Oh, he's not interested.

Alan: Well now, Diane, I'**m open to** suggestions! If Stella here thinks she can help build my muscles and get me **fit**, then I'**m all ears**!

Hank: Great. You both can start your seven-day **trial period** now. Here is some information to look over about our membership **fee** and fitness **finance plan**. Happy training!

(在健身房)

艾　倫：我告訴過妳這裡的音樂就是太大聲。這一整條街都聽得到。

黛　安：這是為了幫你打氣，這樣你才會有活力來使用所有的設備。
　　　　嘿，服務台在那邊。噢，瞧瞧站在後面的那個健美的酷哥！

漢　克：嗨，歡迎光臨「美體世界」。我是漢克。

黛　安：呃……嗨！我們想報名加入一年的會員。

艾　倫：是妳。我只是來這裡……

(一位美女走向艾倫)

史黛拉：嗨，我是史黛拉。我是這裡的私人教練。我能幫忙滿足您所有
　　　　的訓練需求。

黛　安：噢，他沒興趣。

艾　倫：嗯，等等，黛安，我可是廣納建言的！如果史黛拉認為她能幫
　　　　我鍛鍊肌肉、強健體魄，我願意洗耳恭聽！

漢　克：太好了。兩位馬上就可以開始七天的試用期。這兒有一些關於
　　　　我們會員收費和健身財務規劃的資料可參閱。祝您鍛鍊愉快！

 Words & Phrases

1. pump [pʌmp] *v.* 打氣；鼓舞

2. hunky [ˋhʌŋkɪ] *adj.* 肌肉健美的

3. be open to 願意接受……

4. fit [fɪt] *adj.* 健壯的；健康的；
　 適當的；相稱的

5. be all ears 洗耳恭聽

6. trial period [ˋtraɪəl ˏpɪrɪəd] *n.* 試用期

7. fee [fi] *n.* 費用；收費

8. finance plan [ˋfaɪnæns ˏplæn] *n.*
　 財務規劃

活力金句 Pop-up Q&A

■ 你可能會想問…

CDI-08

【置物櫃可租嗎？】

你： Can I rent a personal locker so I can keep some things here?
我可不可以租個私人置物櫃好把一些東西放在這兒？

員工： No. We only have **daily-use** lockers.
不行。我們只提供單日使用的置物櫃。

【可以來幾次？】

你： How many times a week can I come to the gym with my membership?
以我的會員資格，一星期能夠來健身房幾次？

員工： You have the gold pass so you have **unlimited** access.
您有金卡，所以不限次數。

【器材不會用怎麼辦？】

你： I'm unsure about how to use some of the **equipment**. How can I learn?
我不確定某些器材怎麼用。我要怎麼才知道呢？

員工： We have **information sheets** for each **piece** of equipment, or you can ask any one of the floor **staff**.
我們每件器材都有說明書，或者您可以詢問任何一位該樓層的員工。

■ 你可能會想說…

【想打退堂鼓】

你：　I have had enough! I'm never going to the gym again!
　　　我受夠了！我再也不會上健身房了！

朋友：What's wrong? Maybe I can help.
　　　怎麼回事？也許我幫得上忙。

【沒時間運動】

你：　I'm not in a very good mood. I have had no time for exercise all week.
　　　我心情不怎麼好。我已經一整個星期都沒有時間運動了。

朋友：Why don't I get **groceries** and cook dinner tonight so you can go to the gym!
　　　不如今晚換我去買東西、煮晚餐，這樣你就可以上健身房了！

 Words & Phrases

1. daily use 單日使用

2. unlimited [ʌnˋlɪmɪtɪd] *adj.* 無限的

3. equipment [ɪˋkwɪpmənt] *n.* 設備

4. information sheet [ˌɪnfɚˋmeʃən ˌʃit]
　 n. 說明書

5. piece [pis] *n.* 一件（物品）

6. staff [stæf] *n.* 員工（全體）

7. grocery [ˋgrosərɪ] *n.* 日用品；雜物

健美英文很有聊
Healthy **L**iving

健美加油站 Inspiration Lounge

■ 人體地圖 **Body Map**

　　了解自己的身體。如果你能說清楚想鍛鍊哪裡，教練就能幫你盡快達成目標。

neck
[nɛk]
頸部

shoulder
[`ʃoldə]
肩膀

forearm
[`fɔrarm]
前臂

back
[bæk]
背部

upper arm
[`ʌpə͵arm]
上臂

buttocks
[`bʌtəks]
臀部

stomach
[`stʌmək]
腹部

gluteus
[`glu͵tiəs]
臀肌

hamstring
[`hæm͵strɪŋ]
腿後腱

calf
[kæf]
小腿

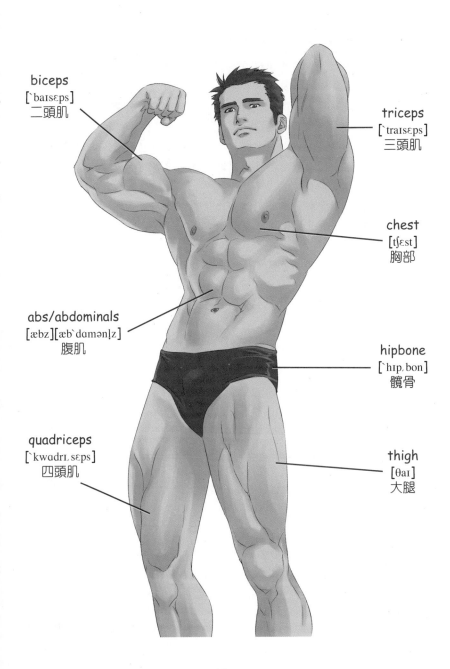

biceps
[ˋbaɪsɛps]
二頭肌

triceps
[ˋtraɪsɛps]
三頭肌

chest
[tʃɛst]
胸部

abs/abdominals
[æbz][æbˋdamənḷz]
腹肌

hipbone
[ˋhɪpˌbon]
髖骨

quadriceps
[ˋkwɑdrɪˌsɛps]
四頭肌

thigh
[θaɪ]
大腿

■ 找對健身房 Finding the Right One

受到激勵想加入健身房了嗎？很好！現在到了最難的部分——具體行動。為了確保你會常上健身房，要確定健身設備符合你的需要。如果地點不方便、健身房太擁擠、或課程時間和你的行程有衝突，乾脆把會員卡扔了，因為你根本不會去用它。簽署任何文件前記得先看過細節部份。我們常聽到有人說：「我想取消健身中心會員資格，但合約上說我不能！」所以簽約前一定要弄清楚以下這些重要的問題：

1. 最短的會期多長？
2. 我必須一次繳費，還是可以按次付費？
3. 我可以終止會員權限或轉讓給朋友嗎？
4. 如果可以，要繳付罰款嗎？

最重要的是，問問你自己：「這家健身房符合我的需求嗎？」

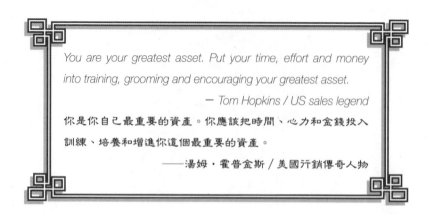

You are your greatest asset. Put your time, effort and money into training, grooming and encouraging your greatest asset.

— *Tom Hopkins / US sales legend*

你是你自己最重要的資產。你應該把時間、心力和金錢投入訓練、培養和增進你這個最重要的資產。

——湯姆‧霍普金斯／美國行銷傳奇人物

Chapter 2

Building the Body
猛男不是一天造成的

別再說「但是」了──腰部的游泳圈並不可愛，身體鬆弛的部位只適合當笑話裡的笑點。但是，在一個大多數工作都在辦公桌上完成、人們幾乎沒有半點運動機會的時代，我們如何趕走討厭的肥肉、保持健康呢？對一些人來說，肌力訓練就是這個問題的答案。這是維持健康、強壯，保持良好氣色的可靠方法。

CDI-10

No buts about it — love handles are not cute and the only room for flabby body parts is in the punch line of a joke. But how in a day and age where most jobs are done from a desk, giving us little chance for exercise, do we keep unwanted fat away and stay healthy? Strength training, for some people, is the answer. It is a reliable way of staying fit, strong and looking good.

基本行話 The Lingo

CDI-11

❶ dumbbell [ˈdʌmˌbɛl]	啞鈴 *n.*
❷ bench [bɛntʃ]	舉重床 *n.* 仰臥推舉 *v.*
❸ barbell [ˈbɑrˌbɛl]	槓鈴 *n.*
❹ spotter [ˈspɑtɚ]	輔助員 *n.*
❺ weight belt [ˈwet ˌbɛlt]	負重帶 *n.*
❻ resistance band [rɪˈzɪstəns ˌbænd]	阻力帶 *n.*
❼ circuit training [ˈsɜkɪt ˌtrenɪŋ]	循環訓練 *n.*
❽ anaerobic [ˌæneəˈrobɪk]	無氧的 *adj.*
❾ aerobic [ˌeəˈrobɪk]	有氧的 *adj.*
❿ rep / repetition [rɛp] [ˌrɛpɪˈtɪʃən]	反覆；重覆 *n.*

暖身練習 Word Workout

CDI-12

A: I'm going to lift **dumbbells** for a while.
B: I will join you. There is a wait to use the **bench** and **barbells**.

A: 我要去舉一下啞鈴。
B: 我跟你去吧。要用舉重床和槓鈴得等一下。

A: You can't **bench** that much!
B: I want to try. Will you be my **spotter**?

A: 你臥舉不了那麼重！
B: 我想試試看。你當我的輔助員好嗎？

A: Should I keep my **weight belt** on while I use a **resistance band**?
B: It is up to you. Do what is most comfortable.

A: 我使用阻力帶時該戴著負重帶嗎？
B: 看你。怎麼樣最舒服就怎麼做。

A: I want to start **circuit training**. I heard it is a great way to get an **anaerobic** and **aerobic** workout.
B: Just remember: your circuit should have 10-12 exercises, and you should do 10-15 **reps** of each exercise.

A: 我想開始做循環訓練。聽說那是進行無氧和有氧運動的絕佳方法。
B: 只要記得：你的循環訓練應該包括十到十二種運動，每種重覆做十到十五下。

健美會話 1　　　　Talk the Talk

CDI-13

(At Jerry's house)

Alan: Sorry, man, I've got to go. I have an early morning tomorrow.

Jerry: Good news, dude. Tomorrow's Sunday! You don't need to get up until at least two, when the game starts.

Alan: I have an appointment with Stella.

Jerry: That's **rough**. I hope that all of those **squats** and **lunges pay off** for you. You would never catch me at the gym.

Alan: I said that once. Now I'm on the road to **Studville**. I'll be so **ripped** you can **bounce** a coin off me.

Jerry: Oh, I plan on getting **ripped** too. Pass me another beer.

Alan: Wait until we hit the beach. You will be so jealous of my **six-pack**. Plus, I'll be much more fit for beach volleyball than you.

Jerry: First of all, I'm retiring to the **sidelines** this year so I'll have a better view of the babes, and I *also* have a **six-pack**. It's getting cold in the **fridge**.

（在傑瑞家）

艾倫：抱歉，我得走了。我明天要早起呢。

傑瑞：好消息，老兄。明天是星期天！你至少可以睡到下午兩點，等比賽開始再起來。

艾倫：我和史黛拉有約。

傑瑞：真辛苦。我希望你做的那些大腿蹲舉和弓箭步會有成果。你就絕不可能在健身房看到我。

艾倫：我也說過那樣的話，但我現在正朝猛男之路邁進。我會變得肌肉暴張，你向我丟硬幣還會彈出去咧。

傑瑞：喔，我也打算讓我自己暴醉呢。再拿罐啤酒給我。

艾倫：咱們到海邊的時候走著瞧。你會忌妒死我的六塊肌。再說呢，我玩沙灘排球會比你稱頭多了。

傑瑞：首先呢，今年本人將退到界外去，這樣我看美眉的視野會比較好。再來，我也有六塊（罐）啊，正在冰箱冰著呢。

 Words & Phrases

1. rough [rʌf] *adj.* 艱苦的

2. squat [skwɑt] *n.* 蹲；半蹲；蹲舉

3. lunge [lʌndʒ] *n.* 弓箭步

4. pay off 【口】回報

5. Studville [ˋstʌdˏvɪl] *n.*
   男子精壯勇猛的狀態
   （stud [stʌd] *n.* 種馬，比喻「精力旺盛的男子」；-ville [-vɪl] *suf.* 表示「……地方」）

6. ripped [rɪpd] *adj.* 肌肉發達突出的；喝醉酒的

7. bounce [baʊns] *v.* 彈回；跳起

8. six-pack [ˋsɪksˏpæk] *n.* 腹部結實的六塊肌肉；（一手）六罐裝的飲料

9. (the) sidelines [ˋsaɪdˏlaɪnz] *n.* 界外區域

10. fridge [frɪdʒ] *n.* 冰箱
    (= refrigerator [rɪˋfrɪdʒˏretə])

健美會話2   Walk the Walk

CDI-14

(The next morning)

Stella: OK, the first and most important rule for **strength training** is to do all exercises with perfect **form**.

Alan: How much weight should I be lifting?

Stella: **That's up to you**. You'll know your weight limit after you have done a few **sets**, each with 12 to 15 reps.

Alan: Should I start with **free weights**? I heard using free weights is the quickest way to build **mass**.

Stella: No. I'm going to start you on the machines. I want you to start strengthening your back and **abdominal** muscles.

Alan: But I want to **focus on** my upper arms.

Stella: I **recommend** you begin with **compound movements**, exercises that use more than one **muscle group**. Only advance weight lifters use **isolation exercises**.

Alan: This sounds like a lot of work and time.

Stella: Yes, but I think you'll be happy with the results you see after just a month of training.

Alan: Great. But the question is ... will you?

（隔天早上）

史黛拉：好，肌力訓練首要的原則就是以最正確的姿勢進行所有的練習。

艾　倫：我應該舉多重呢？

史黛拉：看你囉。你做過幾組練習之後就會知道自己的負重限度，每組要做十二到十五下。

艾　倫：我是不是應該從自由重量訓練開始？我聽說做自由重量是增大肌肉最快的方法。

史黛拉：不。我會讓你先從機械器材開始。我要你先開始強化背部及腹部的肌肉。

艾　倫：但是我想集中訓練我的上臂。

史黛拉：我建議你從複合式運動開始，就是會用到一組以上肌群的運動。只有已經進階的舉重人士才做個別部位的鍛鍊。

艾　倫：聽起來似乎費力又耗時。

史黛拉：沒錯，但是我想只要經過一個月的訓練，你就會對結果感到高興的。

艾　倫：太棒了。但問題是……這會讓妳高興嗎？

 Words & Phrases

1. strength training [ˈstrɛŋθ ˌtrenɪŋ] n. 肌力訓練

2. form [fɔrm] n. 姿勢；形式

3. That's up to you. 由你決定。

4. set [sɛt] n. （一）組；（一）套

5. free weight [ˈfri ˌwet] n. 自由重量舉重

6. mass [mæs] n. 團；塊（在此指肌肉）

7. abdominal [æbˈdɑmənəl] adj. 腹部的

8. focus on 專注於……

9. recommend [ˌrɛkəˈmɛnd] v. 推薦；建議

10. compound movement [ˈkɑmˌpaʊnd ˈmuvmənt] n. 複合式運動

11. isolation exercise [ˌaɪsˈleʃən ˌɛksəsaɪz] n. 針對特定部位的鍛鍊

活力金句 Pop-up Q&A

■ 你可能會想問……

CDI-15

【到底該做幾下？】

你： How many reps should I do?
我應該做幾下？

教練： It depends on what your goal is. Do you want strength, endurance, mass or **tone**?
那要看你的目標是什麼。你想要的是肌力、肌耐力、肌塊或肌張力？

【不想變成肌肉男怎麼辦？】

你： How do I strengthen and **tone** without building mass?
我要如何加強肌力和肌張力，但不要讓肌肉變大？

教練： You need to lift less weight and **increase** your reps.
你需要舉輕一點的重量，並增加次數。

【「週期」是啥米碗糕？】

你： What does "periodize" mean?
「設定週期」是什麼意思呢？

教練： It refers to having **steady progress** in your workout, which helps **prevent injury** and keeps your body **stimulated**.
那是指讓你的訓練循序漸進，那樣有助於避免受傷，並能讓你的身體持續受到刺激。

■ 你也許會想說……

【健美是急不來的】

某人： I feel so **frustrated**. I don't think I'm fit to be a **bodybuilder**.
我覺得好洩氣。我不認為我夠壯可以當健美先生。

你： Are you crazy? Why do you think that as soon as you started lifting, Arnold got into politics?
你瘋了啊？你以為為什麼你一開始舉重，阿諾就只好去搞政治了呢？

【你已經夠健美啦！】

某人： I need to be more fit.
我得再更健壯一點。

你： You are so fit that just looking at you makes me feel healthier.
你已經健壯到我光是看著你就感覺變得更健康了。

Words & Phrases

1. tone [ton] n. 肌張力；v. 加強

2. increase [ɪn`kris] v. 增加；提高

3. steady [`stɛdɪ] adj. 穩定的；平穩的

4. progress [`progrɛs] n. 進展

5. prevent [prɪ`vɛnt] v. 避免

6. injury [`ɪnjɜrɪ] n. 傷害；受傷

7. stimulate [`stɪmulet] v. 刺激

8. frustrated [`frʌstretɪd] adj. 沮喪的

9. bodybuilder [`bʌdɪˏbɪldə] n. 健美人士

健美加油站 Inspiration Lounge

■ 備用辭彙 Vocab Booster

以下這些都是健身房常見的器材和設備，你知道英文怎麼說嗎？

【常見健身用具】

spring collar [ˋsprɪŋ ˌkɑlə] 彈簧環

plate [plet] 金屬板

bar [bɑr] 橫槓

weight lifting gloves [ˋwet ˌlɪftɪŋ ˌglʌvz] 舉重手套

ankle/wrist/hand weight [ˋæŋkḷ/ˋrɪst/ˋhænd ˌwet]

腳踝 / 手腕 / 手部負重帶

medicine ball [ˋmɛdəsṇ ˌbɔl] 藥球

【各式阻力訓練器材】

shoulder press [ˋʃoldə ˌprɛs] 肩部推舉機

chest press [ˋtʃɛst ˌprɛs] 胸部推舉機

pectoral fly [ˋpɛktərəl ˌflaɪ] 蝴蝶式擴胸訓練器

triceps extension [ˋtraɪsɛps ɪkˌstɛnʃən] 三頭肌伸展機

biceps curl [ˋbaɪsɛps ˌkɝl] 二頭肌訓練機

lateral raise [ˋlætərəl ˌrez] 臂部外展機

lat pulldown [ˋlæt ͵pʊldaʊn] 直臂下拉機

leg extension [ˋlɛg ɪkˏstɛnʃən] 大腿伸展機

leg curl [ˋlɛg ͵kɝl] 腿部彎曲機

hip abductor [ˋhɪp æbˏdʌktɚ] 臀部外展機

seated row [ˋsitɪd ͵ro] 坐姿划船機

torso rotation [ˋtɔrso roˏteʃən] 腰部旋轉訓練機.

別找藉口！ No Excuses!

你說你沒時間上健身房？不想花錢買器材，而且也沒地方放？別在找藉口啦，你可以做的運動可多著呢！許多運動非常簡單、隨處可做，而且不用花錢！像仰臥起坐、伏地挺身這些簡單的運動，能幫你隨時隨地強健身體。或許你沒辦法做太多下，但你可以由少量開始，然後慢慢增加。例如，從做十下（或任何你覺得最舒服輕鬆的次數）仰臥起坐開始。做個三回合，每回間隔三十到六十秒的休息時間。你可以每天增加十下。健身沒有捷徑——每個人都必須透過辛苦鍛鍊才能增強體能。你知道嗎？小甜甜布蘭妮每天都要做一百下的仰臥起坐！

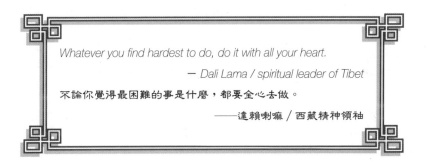

Whatever you find hardest to do, do it with all your heart.

— *Dali Lama / spiritual leader of Tibet*

不論你覺得最困難的事是什麼，都要全心去做。

——達賴喇嘛／西藏精神領袖

Chapter 3

Keep Fit with Cardio
強健心肺保持身材

心肺功能運動是獲得健康最方便且最多樣式的方法之一。無論你是在跑步機上或是走路去商店，你的身體都在燃燒卡路里。不管在不在健身房裡，我們大多數人的日常作息都包含某種形式的心肺功能運動。關鍵在於要有所認識並加以強化。不論是走路、騎腳踏車、跳舞或游泳，你都可以想想如何利用各種不同的方法，在你的日常生活中幫健康加分。

CDI-17

Cardiovascular exercise is one of the most accessible and versatile ways of attaining fitness. Your body burns calories regardless if you are on the treadmill or walking to the store. In or out of the gym most of us include some form of cardio exercise in our daily routine. The key is to recognize it and then maximize it. Be it walking, bicycling, dancing or swimming, consider the various ways to add fitness to your daily life.

基本行話  The Lingo

❶ moderate [ˈmɑdərɪt]	中等的;適度的;溫和的 *adj.*
❷ cardio / cardiovascular [ˈkɑrdɪo] [ˌkɑrdɪoˈvæskjələ]	心臟(血管)的 *adj.*
❸ calorie [ˈkælərɪ]	卡路里 *n.*
❹ vigorous [ˈvɪgərəs]	強而有力的;精力旺盛的 *adj.*
❺ heartbeat [ˈhɑrtˌbit]	心跳 *n.*
❻ endurance [ɪnˈdjurəns]	(忍)耐力;持久力 *n.*
❼ gasp [gæsp]	喘氣;喘不過氣 *v.*
❽ oxygen [ˈɑksədʒən]	氧氣 *n.*
❾ metabolism [məˈtæblˌɪzəm]	新陳代謝 *n.*
❿ stamina [ˈstæmənə]	精力;活力;耐力 *n.*

暖身練習 Word Workout

CDI-19

A: I think I will do a **moderate cardio** workout today.
B: But you said you wanted to shed pounds. You will burn more **calories** if you do a **vigorous** workout.

A: 我想我今天做個溫和的心肺運動好了。
B: 但是你說你想減個幾磅。如果你做激烈運動的話，會消耗更多卡路里。

A: These cardio machines are great!
B: Yeah. They have a device to monitor your **heartbeat**.

A: 這些心肺功能訓練機真棒！
B: 是啊，上面還有儀器可以監測你的心跳。

A: I want to test my **endurance** level. Want to go for a jog?
B: Are you joking? I **gasp** for **oxygen** just going to the corner store!

A: 我想測試我的耐力程度。要不要去慢跑？
B: 你在開玩笑嗎？我光是去轉角的商店就上氣不接下氣了！

A: I have a high **metabolism** so I burn up calories easily.
B: Your **stamina** level ... *(huff huff)* ... is also high. Slow down!

A: 我的新陳代謝率高，所以可以輕易消耗掉卡路里。
B: 你精力充沛的程度……（喘氣）……也很高。速度放慢點啦！

健美會話 1　　　Talk the Talk

CDI-20

(At Alan's house)

Diane: I haven't seen you at the club for a few days. Are you still going?

Alan: Yes. Well, kind of. The last time I saw Stella I felt a little **overwhelmed** by the **fitness jargon**, not to mention that I'm totally **pooped**.

Diane: Why don't you explain that to her? And don't worry about feeling tired. If you **keep to** your plan, your endurance level will increase.

Alan: I guess you're right.

Diane: Don't worry, everyone has tough periods. Just focus on something that keeps you **motivated**. I'm going for a cardio workout right now. Why don't you come along?

Alan: Any chance I have to get hot and sweaty with you I'll take!

Diane: Get your mind out of the **gutter** and back on the fitness **track**.

Alan: Hey! You're the one that said to focus on something that motivates me!

（在艾倫家）

黛安：我已經幾天沒在俱樂部看到你了。你還有去嗎？

艾倫：有。嗯，算有吧。上回我見到史黛拉的時候，我覺得有點被健身術語給打敗了，更別提我整個人都累翻了。

黛安：你怎麼不跟她明說呢？還有，不用擔心會覺得累。如果你遵循你的計畫，你的耐力就會增加。

艾倫：我想妳說的對。

黛安：別擔心，每個人都得經歷辛苦的階段。只要專注在能激勵你的東西上就好了。我現在要去做心肺運動了。你何不一起來呢？

艾倫：任何能和妳一起發熱流汗的機會我都會把握的！

黛安：別想歪了，回到健身的正題上。

艾倫：嘿！是妳說要專注在能激勵我的東西上的！

 Words & Phrases

1. overwhelm [ˏovɚˋhwɛlm] *v.*
   擊潰；壓倒

2. fitness jargon [ˋfɪtnɪs ˏdʒɑrgən] *n.*
   健身術語

3. pooped [pupt] *adj.* 精疲力盡的

4. keep to 固守；遵循

5. motivate [ˋmotəˏvet] *v.*
   激勵；使產生動機

6. gutter [ˋgʌtɚ] *n.* 陰溝；
   此處指「下流的心態」

7. track [træk] *n.* 足跡；軌轍；路線

健美會話2　　Walk the Walk

CDI-21

(At the Club)

Diane: After we **warm up** let's go on the **cross-trainer**.

Alan:　Sounds good. Diane! What are you doing?

Diane: What? Oh, just the **splits**. Look I can do them like this. And like this and ...

Alan:　Wow! You are so **flexible**. I can barely touch my toes.

Diane: Well, keep working out and your **flexibility** will improve. Ready for the machines?

Alan:　Sure am. Let me see. It says to choose the course I want. **Beginner**? Ha ha, no way. This is more like it — **intense** mountain climb.

Diane: You should take it easy. It's your first time.

Alan:　Watch and learn, young **grasshopper**. At the end when you read my **distance**, speed and calories burned, you'll wish you went harder too.

*(Ten minutes later. Alan is **panting** and **slumped** over the machine.)*

Diane: Oh, wise fitness **guru**, I have watched and I have learned. I learned never to do what you just did!

(在俱樂部)

黛安：做完暖身之後，咱們去用交叉訓練機吧。

艾倫：聽起來不錯。黛安！妳在做什麼？

黛安：什麼？喔，就劈腿嘛。你看我可以像這樣做。還可以這樣，還有
　　　……

艾倫：哇！妳的柔軟度真好。我只能勉強碰到腳趾頭。

黛安：嗯，繼續鍛鍊下去，你的柔軟度就會改善。準備上訓練機了嗎？

艾倫：當然。我看看。上面說，選擇我想要的訓練。初級？哈哈，怎麼
　　　可能。這個才像樣——高強度登山模式。

黛安：你別心急，這是你的第一次。

艾倫：讓妳見識一下吧，小蚱蜢。等妳最後看到我的距離、速度和消耗
　　　的卡路里，妳會希望自己也更努力點的。

(十分鐘後，艾倫氣喘吁吁倒在訓練機上)

黛安：喔，睿智的健身大師，我已經見識到了。我學到絕對不要重蹈你
　　　的覆轍！

Words & Phrases

1. warm up 做暖身運動

2. cross-trainer [ˋkrɔs͵trenɚ] *n.*
   交叉訓練機

3. split [splɪt] *n.* 劈開；劈腿

4. flexible [ˋflɛksəbl̩] *adj.*
   柔軟的；有彈性的

5. beginner [bɪˋgɪnɚ] *n.* 初學者

6. intense [ɪnˋtɛns] *adj.* 強烈的；激烈的

7. distance [ˋdɪstəns] *n.* 距離

8. grasshopper [ˋgræs͵hɑpɚ] *n.* 蚱蜢
   (電視影集「功夫」中，功夫大師以 "young
   grasshopper" 稱少年時期的男主角)

9. pant [pænt] *v.* 喘氣

10. slump [slʌmp] *v.* 癱倒；暴跌

11. guru [ˋguru] *n.* 大師

活力金句 QA Pop-up Q&A

你可能會想問······ CDI-22

【伸展操有必要嗎?】

你： Do I really need to **stretch** after my workout?
我運動後真的需要伸展身體嗎?

教練： Yes! If you don't, you will lose **flexibility** and **range of motion**.
是的!如果你不做,會喪失柔軟度和關節活動度。

【怎樣效果最好?】

你： How do I know if I'm getting the most from my workouts?
我怎麼知道我達到運動的最大效果了?

教練： You should use a heart **monitor**. It will help you stay in your **target zone**.
你應該用心臟監視器,它會幫助你維持在目標區內。

【啥米是「目標區」?】

你： What does "target zone" mean?
「目標區」是什麼意思?

教練： It is the **intensity** level of your workout. The target zone for losing weight is different than that for building strength.
目標區是指你的運動強度級數。減重和增強體能的目標區不一樣。

你也許會想說……

【有心最重要】

朋友： I've got to find an exercise to help me look better.
我得找一種運動來幫助我，讓我看起來更好。

你： **Positive** thinking always helps.
積極的思考永遠有幫助。

【你好努力喔！】

你： Wow! You are the cardio queen.
哇！妳真是心肺運動皇后。

某人： Thanks. I have been training hard.
謝啦，我一直在努力鍛鍊。

 Words & Phrases

1. stretch [strɛtʃ] v. 伸展

2. flexibility [ˌflɛksəˋbɪlətɪ] n.
柔軟度；彈性

3. range of motion [ˋrendʒ əf ˋmoʃən] n.
關節活動程度

4. monitor [ˋmɑnətə] n. 監視器

5. target zone [ˋtɑrgɪt ˌzon] n. 目標區

6. intensity [ɪnˋtɛnsətɪ] n. 強度；激烈

7. positive [ˋpɑzətɪv] adj.
正面的；積極的

健美加油站 Inspiration Lounge

■ 備用辭彙 Vocab Booster　　CDI-23

經常健身的人對以下器材應該不陌生吧？你知道它們的英文怎麼說嗎？

【常見健身用具】

pedometer [pɪˋdɑmətɚ] 計步器

calories counter [ˋkælərɪs ˏkaʊntɚ] 卡路里計算器

body fat tester [ˋbɑdɪ ˏfæt ˏtɛstɚ] 體脂肪測定儀

heart rate monitor [ˋhɑrt ˏret ˏmɑnətɚ] 心律監視器

jump rope [ˋdʒʌmp ˏrop] 跳繩

trampoline [ˋtræmpəˏlɪn] 彈簧墊

treadmill [ˋtrɛdˏmɪl] 跑步機

elliptical trainer [ɪˋlɪptɪkl ˋtrenɚ]（= cross-trainer）橢圓軌道機

free climber [ˋfri ˏklaɪmɚ]（= stair climber）踩踏機

step master [ˋstɛp ˏmæstɚ] 踏步機

■ 跑步機面板 Treadmill Console

跑步機是常見的健身器材之一。許多跑步機都是歐美進口，面板上都是英文說明。把下面的單字記起來，以後就不會霧煞煞囉！

卡路里數

每小時燃燒的卡路里數

傾斜度

跑步

慢跑

步行

速度

步數

檢視

圈數計算

CALORIES

CALORIES/HOUR

INCLINE

RUN

JOG

WALK

SPEED

PACE

SCAN

LAP COUNTER

HEART RATE

TIME

DISTANCE

TIME

TEMPERATURE

WEIGHT

HEARTBEAT

心律

時間

距離

時間

體溫

體重

心跳

START

STOP

ENTER

SPEED

INCLINE

速度控制

啟動

停止

進入

傾斜度控制

【跑步機訓練模式】

Fitness test　20min 體能測試模式

Weight Loss　45min 減重模式

Cardiovascular　30min 心肺功能模式

Speed Challenge　30min 加速模式

Express　15min 速跑模式

Speed Interval 間歇模式

Pikes Peak　20min 越野賽跑模式

5 Kilometer Run 五公里路跑模式

Custom Programs 手動設定

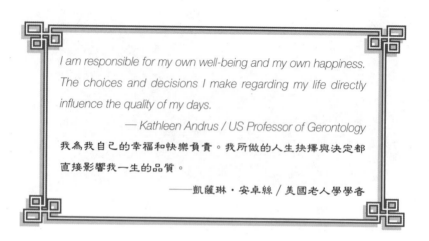

I am responsible for my own well-being and my own happiness. The choices and decisions I make regarding my life directly influence the quality of my days.

— Kathleen Andrus / US Professor of Gerontology

我為我自己的幸福和快樂負責。我所做的人生抉擇與決定都直接影響我一生的品質。

——凱薩琳‧安卓絲 / 美國老人學學者

MEMO

Chapter 4

Back to Class
一起跳出健康美麗

一、二、三、四。噢,在我倒地前請停下來吧!試著跟上活力四射的教練,卻老是絆到自己的腳,這樣的記憶以往一直讓你對健美班望而卻步。感謝老天,時代已經變了!如今,加入課程就可以鍛鍊身體、學習舞蹈新招、重溫拳擊技巧,或舒展筋骨放鬆一下。現在就報名吧!

CDI-24

One and two and three and four. Oh please stop before I fall on the floor! Memories of tripping over your own feet while trying to keep up with perky instructors used to discourage you from taking fitness classes. Thank goodness times have changed! Today when you join a class you can get fit, learn new dance moves, brush up on boxing skills or stretch and relax. Sign up now!

基本行話 The Lingo

❶ intermediate [ˌɪntɚˋmidɪət]	中級的 *adj.*	
❷ advanced [ədˋvænst]	高級的；進階的 *adj.*	
❸ low-/high-impact [ˋlo-/ˋhaɪˋɪmpækt]	低 / 高衝擊性的 *adj.*	
❹ multi-level [ˌmʌltɪˋlɛvl]	多種程度的 *adj.*	
❺ studio [ˋstjudɪˌo]	練習室（舞蹈）； 工作室（攝影、繪畫等）*n.*	
❻ cool-down [ˋkulˌdaʊn]	緩和運動 *n.*	
❼ body conditioning [ˋbɑdɪ kənˌdɪʃənɪŋ]	身體健整 *n.*	
❽ instructor [ɪnˋstrʌktɚ]	指導者；講師 *n.*	
❾ exercise ball [ˋɛksɚˌsaɪz ˌbɔl]	健身球 *n.*	
❿ exercise mat [ˋɛksɚˌsaɪz ˌmæt]	運動墊 *n.*	

暖身練習 Word Workout

CDI-26

A: What class do you want to join and at what level? Beginner, **intermediate** or **advanced**?

B: Do you offer a **low-impact**, **multi-level** aerobics class?

A: 你想參加什麼課程，哪一級？初級、中級或高級？

B: 你們有沒有開低衝擊性、適合各種程度的有氧課程呢？

A: The class is in the fourth **studio** down the hall.

B: Thanks. Am I in time for the warm-up?

A: 那一班在走廊那邊第四間教室。

B: 謝謝。我趕得上做暖身嗎？

A: Many people forget how important the **cool-down** is.

B: You're right. It's as important as the warm-up.

A: 很多人都忘了緩和運動有多重要。

B: 你說的對。它跟暖身運動一樣重要。

A: This class is great. It focuses on total **body conditioning**.

B: I know. And I love how the **instructor** uses the **exercise ball** and **exercise mat**.

A: 這堂課真棒。它著重的是全身的健整。

B: 我知道。我非常喜歡教練運用健身球和運動墊的方式。

 健美會話 1  Talk the Talk

(Alan and Diane are eating lunch.)

Alan: Stella is starting me on a workout program that will make me a **lean**, **mean** muscle machine.

Diane: I'll believe it when I see it. While you are becoming Mr. Universe, I'll be **slimming down** in an **aerobics** class.

Alan: Are you going to take a **step class**?

Diane: No. I am thinking about taking **hip hop**. Do you know that you can **burn** 120 calories by dancing for 20 minutes?

Alan: Maybe. But learning hip hop isn't **practical**. You can burn almost the same number of calories by digging a hole. Why don't you plant a garden or something?

Diane: Great idea, but how about I leave the digging for you? Then I can watch you **flex** your new muscles as you dig!

Alan: Ha ha. So when is your first fitness class?

Diane: In an hour. That's why I'm eating such a **light** lunch.

Alan: Um ... Diane, I don't think cream sauce over **pasta** and corn soup is considered a light lunch!

（艾倫和黛安正在吃午餐）

艾倫：史黛拉要開始讓我進行一套會把我變成一個無贅肉猛男的健身計畫。

黛安：等我親眼看到才相信。在你變身成環球先生的同時，我會在有氧課中苗條下來。

艾倫：妳要去上階梯有氧嗎？

黛安：不是。我想去上嘻哈有氧。你知道跳二十分鐘可以燃燒一百二十卡嗎？

艾倫：或許吧。但是學有氧嘻哈不實際。挖土坑也可以燃燒差不多的熱量。妳幹嘛不去種花園呀什麼的？

黛安：好主意，但是挖土坑這種事兒留給你來做怎麼樣？那我就可以在你挖的時候看你炫耀新長的肌肉了！

艾倫：哈哈。那妳第一堂健身課是什麼時候？

黛安：再一個小時。這正是為什麼我吃這麼清淡的午餐。

艾倫：嗯……，黛安，我想奶油義大利麵和玉米濃湯不算是清淡的午餐吧！

 Words & Phrases

1. lean [lin] *adj.* 瘦的；脂肪少的

2. mean [min] *adj.* 【俚】出色的；很棒的

3. slim down 瘦下來

4. aerobics [ˌeəˋrobɪks] *n.* 有氧運動

5. step class [ˋstɛp ˌklæs] *n.* 階梯（有氧）課程

6. hip hop [ˋhɪp ˌhɑp] *n.* 嘻哈（有氧）

7. burn [bɝn] *v.* 燃燒；消耗

8. practical [ˋpræktɪkl̩] *adj.* 實用的；實際的

9. flex [flɛks] *v.* 收縮（肌肉）；flex one's muscles 展示某人的力量

10. light [laɪt] *adj.* 輕的；清淡的；不油膩的

11. pasta [ˋpɑstə] *n.* 義大利麵食（如通心粉、義大利麵、千層麵等）

健美會話2　Walk the Walk

CDI-28

(In the hip hop class)

Diane: Hi. This is my first time in your class.

Teacher: Great. Find a place close to the front so you can watch me. We'll be starting in just a minute.

Diane: Thanks.

(Teacher turns on the music.)

Teacher: OK. Everyone, **follow** me! To the side. Stretch those arms. Feel it! Love it! One and two and three. That's right, **great work**!

Diane: *(thinking to herself)* Wow, this is hard. I can't **keep up with** her.

Teacher: Great warm-up. Now move it a little faster.

Diane: That was just the warm-up!?

Teacher: *(to Diane)* Excuse me, are you OK? You look just a little **pale**.

Diane: This is just a little harder than I thought.

Teacher: Did you find the intermediate class this difficult?

Diane: I never took it. This is my first exercise class ever.

Teacher: Honey, this is the advanced class. You should be in the beginner class!

（在有氧嘻哈班）

黛安：嗨，這是我第一次上您的課。

老師：很好。找個靠近前面的位置，這樣妳才看得到我。我們等會兒就要開始囉。

黛安：謝謝。

（老師放音樂）

老師：好。大家跟著我！向側面。伸展手臂。感覺它！愛上它！一、二、三。就是這樣，做得很好！

黛安：*（心裡想著）*哇，好難喔。我跟不上她。

老師：很好的暖身。現在動作加快一點。

黛安：那只是暖身啊！？

老師：*（對黛安）*對不起，妳還好嗎？妳的臉色看起來有點發白。

黛安：這比我想像的困難了一些。

老師：妳覺得之前的中級班也這麼難嗎？

黛安：我從來沒上過中級班。這是我這輩子的第一堂健身課。

老師：親愛的，這是高級班。妳應該去上初級班！

 Words & Phrases

1. Great work! 做得很好！

2. follow [ˋfɑlo] *v.* 跟隨；跟著

3. keep up with ... 跟上……

4. pale [pel] *adj.* （臉色）蒼白的

活力金句 Pop-up Q&A

■ 也許你會想問……

 CDI-29

【訓練行程怎麼排？】

你： How often should I exercise?
我應該多久運動一次？

教練： You can do at least 30 minutes of cardio three to five times a week as well as two to three **sessions** of strength training.
你一週可以做三到五次、至少三十分鐘的心肺功能運動，以及二到三回的肌力訓練。

【為什麼瘦不下來？】

你： Why am I not losing any weight even though I work out 5 days a week?
我一週運動五天，為什麼體重還是減不下來？

教練： Perhaps you are not working out in your target zone. Or maybe you need to make some changes in your diet.
也許你做的運動並未配合你的目標區。也或許你的飲食必須做點改變。

【低衝擊性運動很遜嗎？】

你： Aren't low-impact workouts for **wimps**?
低衝擊的運動不是給軟腳蝦做的嗎？

教練： Not at all. Low impact is great for people whose bodies can't **handle** the **stress** from activities like **jogging**.
並非如此。對於身體受不了像慢跑這類運動的壓力的人，低衝擊力是很好的。

■ 也許你會想說……

【有運動有差喔！】

朋友： I have started exercising to lose weight.
我開始運動減肥了。

你： That's **fantastic**! I can already see that it's working!
那太好了！我已經看得出效果了！

【在家健身】

朋友： I think I might buy an at-home workout video.
我想我或許會買個家庭用健身錄影帶。

你： That's a very convenient way to **shape up**.
那是健身非常便利的一個方法。

 Words & Phrases

1. session [ˈsɛʃən] *n.* 練習期間；
   活動期間

2. wimp [wɪmp] *n.* 軟弱的人

3. handle [ˈhændl] *v.* 處理；承受

4. stress [strɛs] *n.* 壓力

5. jogging [ˈdʒɑgɪŋ] *n.* 慢跑

6. fantastic [fænˈtæstɪk] *adj.* 極好的

7. shape up 改善身體狀況

健美加油站 Inspiration Lounge

健身中心常見的有氧課程 Cardio Classes　　CDI-30

看看下列的介紹，找個能讓你精力充沛（pumped）的課程吧！

- 階梯有氧 Step：

  這是踏入刺激的階梯有氧運動的入門課（introduction）。你可以從這堂課學到階梯運動的基本動作。

- 強力階梯有氧 Power step：

  重複上下踏板（raiser）能促進血液循環。你可以好好做一場心肺功能運動，也可以期待擁有迷死人的美腿和翹臀！

- 美體塑身 Body Sculpt：

  這門課程的重點是，你猜對了——雕塑你的身材。運用啞鈴和地板操（floor exercises），幫助你練出凹凸有緻（carved）的身材。

- 爵士有氧 Jazz：

  舞出健康來。結合現代舞（modern dance）和爵士舞（jazz）的動作，帶給你充滿動感、富教育性又超級好玩的運動。

- 戰鬥有氧 Body Combat：

  活力十足而且樂趣多多。當音樂響起時，就運用搏擊動作（kick-boxing）踢出健康與美麗吧！

- 嘻哈有氧 Hip Hop：

  上過這個課程之後，你也能在舞池（dance floor）上嘻哈一下了！既能瘦身，又能跳酷炫的街舞，就是參加這個課程的兩個好理由。

- 熱舞有氧 Body Jam：

  你將在這堂適合各年齡層的有氧運動中隨各種節奏起舞，嘻哈、放客（funk）和拉丁舞（Latin）只是其中幾種而已。

- 飛輪有氧 Spinning：

  上這堂課你得騎上一種固定式腳踏車（stationary bicycle），跟著教練指示做一整套動作。這種腳踏車上裝有飛輪（flywheel），騎起來

比電腦化固定腳踏車更真實。這是當今在健身中心很流行的激烈運動課程。

- 拳擊有氧 Boxercise：
  做拳擊運動的人必須有健康良好的心肺適能（cardio fitness）。拳擊有氧應用專業拳擊手的訓練方式，使你體格強壯、意志堅強。
- 跆擊有氧 Kick Aerobics：
  將武術（martial arts）帶進教室，幫助你在拳打腳踢中達到完美的健康狀態。
- 水中有氧 Aquatic Aerobics：
  隨著音樂在水中做各種體操動作。利用水的阻力（resistance）和浮力（buoyancy），加強心肺功能，兼具健身、塑身和復健的效果。

■ 團體的精神鼓勵 Hang in There!

你自己一人運動無法貫徹到底嗎？那就加入健身課程吧。健身中心的課程本身很有趣，而且如果一個空間中擠滿了全力以赴的人，你置身其中也會被激發出潛能。你會感受到團體能量（group energy），感到辛苦的時候，就利用這股能量鼓勵自己撐下去吧！如果那樣不管用，就找一位身材健美的學員，告訴自己：突破難關後就能變成那個樣子。你還可以仰賴自尊——為了不被其他學員瞧不起，一定要咬緊牙關撐下去！

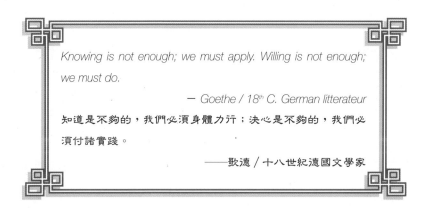

Knowing is not enough; we must apply. Willing is not enough; we must do.

— *Goethe / 18th C. German litterateur*

知道是不夠的，我們必須身體力行；決心是不夠的，我們必須付諸實踐。

——歌德／十八世紀德國文學家

Section Two

Shaping the Soul
休養性靈

2

Chapter 5

Yoga: For Your Body
身心合一的瑜珈 and So

瑜珈,一種四千多年前就發展出來的修行法,現在已經擴展到全球。瑜珈常被誤解為只和身體姿勢有關。事實上,在瑜珈的演化中有被稱為阿斯坦加的八支行法。這八支行法提供了如何過一個有意義、有目標的人生的遵循方針。讓我們拿起我們的墊子向這禁得起時代考驗的修行法——瑜珈——致敬!

CDI-31

Yoga, a practice that was developed over 4,000 years ago, has now stretched itself across the globe. Often yoga is misunderstood to be just about posture. In fact, there are eight limbs called Ashtanga in the yogic path. These eight limbs provide guidelines on how to live a life of meaning and purpose. Let's raise our mats to yoga, a practice that has stood the test of time!

基本行話 The Lingo

CDI-32

❶ sticky mat [ˈstɪkɪ ˌmæt]	止滑墊 *n.*	
❷ foam block [ˈfom ˌblɑk]	輔助磚（瑜珈）*n.*	
❸ hatha [ˈhɑθə]	哈達瑜珈 *n.* （瑜珈八支行法的一種，著重姿勢）	
❹ bikram [ˈbɪkrəm]	熱瑜迦 *n.* （共有二十六式，要在 40℃ 左右的房間裏進行）	
❺ ashtanga [ˈəʃtɑngə]	阿斯坦加 *n.* （指「瑜珈八支行法」）	
❻ pranayama [ˌprɑnəˈyɑmə]	帕那亞瑪 *n.* （呼吸控制法，指瑜珈的「調氣」）	
❼ flow [flo]	流動 *v.*	
❽ asana [əˈsɑnə]	阿色那 *n.* （體位法，指瑜珈的「動作」）	
❾ inhale [ɪnˈhel]	吸氣 *v.*	
❿ exhale [ɛksˈhel]	吐氣 *v.*	

暖身練習 Word Workout

 CDI-33

A: I have joined a yoga class. Should I just bring a **sticky mat**?
B: It would be a good idea to also take a **foam block**.

A: 我參加了瑜珈課。我是不是應該帶個止滑墊呢？
B: 再帶個輔助磚是個好主意。

A: Is **hatha** the original style of yoga?
B: Yes. Many styles have developed since then.

A: 哈達是瑜珈最初的形式嗎？
B: 是的。從那時起發展出了很多形式。

A: How do I know what to choose? **Bikram**, **ashtanga** or power yoga?
B: You can learn a little about each style to discover which one suits you best.

A: 我要怎麼知道該選什麼？熱瑜珈、阿斯坦加，或強力瑜珈？
B: 你可以每種形式都學一點，找出最那一種適合你。

A: How important is **pranayama** in yoga?
B: Very! You should **flow** through each **asana** while slowly **inhaling** and **exhaling**.

A: 呼吸控制法對於瑜珈有多重要呢？
B: 很重要！你應在緩慢吸氣、吐氣的同時，順其自然地做每一個體位。

健美會話 1　Talk the Talk

CDI-34

(Over at Jerry's)

Diane: Jerry!

Jerry: What!?

Diane: You have a book about yoga on your coffee table. Are you **practicing yoga**?

Jerry: Of course not. Do I look like a tree-hugging hippie to you? My sister left it here. She thought I might find it useful.

Diane: So have you found it useful?

Jerry: Well, I have used it as a beer **coaster** a few times. You know, I really should buy some coasters to protect the table ...

Diane: Jerry! Come on – if anyone could use a little **boost** in healthy living, it's you!

Jerry: Tell me how doing **sun salutations** can help a guy like me.

Diane: Well, **meditation** will help you think clearer, and your body could sure use some **conditioning**. You are about as **flexible** as this table!

Jerry: But my body is as **firm** as ...

Diane: As firm as pudding! Jerry, get real. You are a man and you have breasts!

Jerry: I always say four are better than two!

（在傑瑞家）

黛安：傑瑞！

傑瑞：幹嘛！？

黛安：你的咖啡桌上有本關於瑜珈的書。你在練瑜珈嗎？

傑瑞：當然沒有。對你而言，我看起來像是個抱著樹的環保嬉皮嗎？
書是我姐留下來的。她認為我可能會覺得有用。

黛安：那你覺得有用嗎？

傑瑞：嗯，我是有幾次拿它來當啤酒墊。妳知道的，我的確應該買些杯
墊來保護桌面……

黛安：傑瑞！拜託——如果有誰需要增加一點健康的生活，那個人就是
你啦！

傑瑞：告訴我做拜日式如何會對像我這樣的人有幫助。

黛安：嗯，冥想會讓你的思慮更清晰，而你的身體肯定需要一點調整。
你的柔軟度就跟這張桌子差不多！

傑瑞：可是我的身體結實得像……

黛安：結實得像布丁！傑瑞，認清現實吧。你是個男人，卻有胸部！

傑瑞：我常說多多益善嘛！

 Words & Phrases

1. practice yoga 練瑜珈

2. coaster [ˈkostə] n. 杯墊

3. boost [bust] n. 增加；促進

4. sun salutation [ˈsʌn sæljə͵teʃən]
n. 拜日式（瑜珈體位法）

5. meditation [͵mɛdəˋteʃən] n. 冥想

6. conditioning [kənˋdɪʃənɪŋ] n.
調節；調整

7. flexible [ˈflɛksəbl] adj.
柔軟的；有彈性的

8. firm [fɝm] adj. 結實的

健美會話2  Walk the Walk

(The next day in a yoga class)

Diane: I can't believe I **suckered** you into taking yoga.

Jerry: **For the record**, this is a bet. After this one class I will collect my winnings, buy some beer and go back to my couch.

Diane: You never know – you might like how the **postures** feel. First roll out your mat and sit **cross-legged** on it. Then practice your pranayama.

Jerry: Prana what?

Diane: Shh. Just close your eyes and breathe.

(Ten minutes later)

Teacher: Hello everyone. We will do a series of asanas today that will improve **circulation** and **calm** the mind.

Diane: Excuse me, I forgot the right way to breathe.

Teacher: Inhale through your nose and exhale through your mouth. Ah, pardon me, sir. You can open your eyes now. We are beginning.

*(Jerry is **snoring**.)*

Diane: Oh, my God! Jerry, this is so **embarrassing**. Wake up!

Jerry: Wow, you were right. I feel great.

（隔天在瑜珈課中）

黛安：我真不敢相信我把你騙來上瑜珈課了。

傑瑞：我必須聲明，這是打賭。這一堂課之後，我會收取我贏來的錢，
　　　買些啤酒，然後回到我的沙發上。

黛安：你怎麼知道——你也許會喜歡做那些姿勢的感覺。先把你的墊子
　　　攤開，然後盤腿坐在上面。接著練習你的帕那亞瑪。

傑瑞：怕那什麼？

黛安：噓。閉上眼睛呼吸就是了。

（十分鐘之後）

老師：大家好。我們今天會做一系列促進循環、安定心神的體位。

黛安：對不起，我忘記正確的呼吸法了。

老師：用妳的鼻子吸氣，然後用嘴巴吐氣。啊，對不起，先生。你現在
　　　可以睜開眼睛了。我們要開始了。

（傑瑞在打呼）

黛安：噢，我的天啊！傑瑞，這真是太丟人了。醒醒啊！

傑瑞：哇，妳説的沒錯。我覺得好極了。

 Words & Phrases

1. sucker [ˋsʌkə] v.【俚】拐騙

2. for the record 正式公開宣稱

3. posture [ˋpɑstʃə] n. 姿勢

4. cross-legged [ˋkrɔsˋlɛgɪd] adj./adv.
　盤腿的（地）；翹著二郎腿的（地）

5. circulation [ˌsɝkjəˋleʃən] n. 循環

6. calm [kɑm] v. 冷靜；鎮定

7. snore [snor] v. 打鼾

8. embarrassing [ɪmˋbærəsɪŋ] adj.
　令人尷尬的

活力金句 Q A Pop-up Q&A

也許你會想問……

CDI-36

【什麼時候練瑜珈最好？】

你： When is the best time to practice yoga?
練習瑜珈最好的時間是什麼時候？

教練： If you want the **energizing effects**, practice in the morning. If you want **relaxation**, try an evening session.
如果你要的是提神效果，就在早上練。如果你要的是放鬆，那就試試在傍晚的時段做。

【感冒該暫停嗎？】

你： If I have a cold, can I still practice?
如果我感冒了，還是可以練嗎？

教練： **Consult** with your instructor. For some people, stopping until you are better is wise.
問問你的指導老師。對某些人而言，先暫停等到好點時再練是明智之舉。

【「那個」來可以練嗎？】

你： If I have my **period**, should I not practice?
如果我生理期來了，我應該不要練嗎？

教練： You can still practice. With some **poses** you might feel **menstrual pain**, just **sit** those **out**.
你還是可以練。有些姿勢妳可能會感到經痛，那就不要做。

■ 也許你會想說……

【柔軟度很差】

你： I'm too un-flexible. Everyone will laugh at me in the class.
我柔軟度很差。上課大家都會笑我的。

教練： Everyone has different levels. People will only see you trying to **enhance** your life.
每個人程度不同。人們只會看到你是在試圖提升生活品質。

【呼吸配合不起來】

你： I can't get the breathing right for practicing yoga.
我做不好練瑜珈時要配合的呼吸。

教練： Don't worry. With practice you will find it easier.
別擔心。只要練習，你就會覺得容易多了。

Words & Phrases

1. energize [ˋɛnɚˌdʒaɪz] v.
補充能量；使有精力

2. effect [əˋfɛkt] n. 效果

3. relaxation [ˌrilæksˋeʃən] n.
放鬆；鬆弛

4. consult [kənˋsʌlt] v. 諮詢

5. period [ˋpɪrɪəd] n. 生理期；期間

6. pose [poz] n. 姿勢

7. menstrual pain [ˋmɛnstruəl ˌpen]
n. 經痛

8. sit out 坐視；不參加

9. enhance [ɪnˋhæns] v. 增進；提升

健美加油站 Inspiration Lounge

■ 美好的一天從瑜珈開始 Start a Day with Yoga

不是每個人都有時間上瑜珈課，但有些基本的動作自己在家就可以做，例如拜日式（sun salutations）。拜日式包含十二種體位，如果你有練瑜珈，你可能已經學過了。為了平衡你身體的左右兩側，這套動作要做兩次。拜日式能強化體能、增加柔軟度。就像做大多數的瑜珈動作一樣，當你在伸展（stretch）和擴張（extend）身體的時候要吸氣，收縮（contract）或彎曲（fold）身體的時候則要吐氣。

❶ Mountain 山式　　❷ Hands up 展臂式　　❸ Head to knees
前屈式

❼ Upward Dog
上狗式

❹ Lunge 弓箭式

❽ Downward Dog
下狗式

❺ Plank 木板式

❾ Lunge 弓箭式

❻ Stick 棍棒式

❿ Head to knees
前屈式

⓫ Hands up 展臂式

⓬ Mountain 山式

You gotta dance like nobody's watching, dream like you will live forever, live like you're going to die tomorrow and love like it's never going to hurt.

— Meme Grifsters / inspirational speaker

你得像如入無人之境似地起舞，如永生不死般地作夢，像明天就要死去似地過活，並且像永遠不會受傷似地去愛。

——敏敏・葛菲斯特絲／勵志大師

Chapter 6

Retreat for Some
美療舒壓休閒館　R&R

壓力被認為是現代社會中導致身心疾病的主要原因。如果你有幸偶爾接受專業技術的尊寵，不但會看起來氣色不錯，也保證能讓自己擁有更高的生活品質。如果你的荷包不能讓你好好享受一趟水療或休閒舒壓，那就抽空在家給自己一些溫柔的寵愛和呵護吧。

CDI-37

Stress is thought to be a primary cause of physical and mental illness in modern society. If you are lucky enough to receive professional pampering from time to time, you will not only look good, but will insure a better quality of life for yourself. If funds prevent you from being able to enjoy a spa or retreat, take time out at home to give yourself some tender love and care.

 基本行話 The Lingo

CDI-38

❶ hot springs [`hɑt `sprɪŋz]	溫泉（常用複數）*n.*	
❷ massage [mə`sɑʒ]	推拿；按摩 *n.*	
❸ refresh [rɪ`frɛʃ]	提神；重新喚起 *v.*	
❹ steam room [`stim ˏrum]	蒸氣室 *n.*	
❺ hot tub [`hɑt ˏtʌb]	熱水浴桶、浴缸、浴池 *n.*	
❻ sauna [`saʊnə]	三溫暖烤箱室 *n.*	
❼ aesthetician [ˏɛsθə`tɪʃən]	美療師 *n.*	
❽ moisturize [`mɔɪstʃəˏraɪz]	使……有溼氣；增加水分 *v.*	
❾ treatment [`tritmənt]	治療（法）；處理（方式）*n.*	
❿ toxin [`tɔksɪn]	毒素 *n.*	

暖身練習　　Word Workout

A: We went to the **hot springs** last night. Then we had a **massage**.
B: Sounds relaxing. I bet you feel very **refreshed** today.

A: 我們昨晚去泡溫泉，然後還做了按摩。
B: 聽起來蠻放鬆的樣子。我敢說你今天一定感覺神清氣爽。

A: I'm going into the **steam room**. Are you staying in the **hot tub**?
B: No. I want to get dry. I'll be in the **sauna**.

A: 我要去蒸氣室了。你還會待在熱浴池嗎？
B: 不了。我想把身體弄乾。我會在三溫暖烤箱。

A: Your skin looks so much healthier than the last time I saw you.
B: I went to an **aesthetician**. She gave me a **moisturizing treatment**.

A: 你的皮膚看起來比我上次見到你的時候健康多了。
B: 我去找了美容師。她幫我做了保濕護理。

A: Would you recommend soaking in a bath with Epsom salts?
B: Sure. It's a great way to get rid of **toxins** in your body.

A: 你會推薦用瀉鹽泡澡嗎？
B: 當然。那是排除你體內毒素的絕佳方法。

健美會話 1　Talk the Talk

CDI-40

(Jerry and Diane are in a drug store.)

Jerry:　You have examined every bottle on this shelf. What are you looking for?

Diane:　Summer is coming. I want to find a **topical cream** to reduce my **cellulite**.

Jerry:　Sick. I don't want to hear about all those little **sacs** of fat giving you **lumpy** skin!

Diane:　Jerry - you're not helping.

Jerry:　Maybe not, but my mom might be able to. She is an aesthetician.

Diane:　Really? Does she work in a **salon**? I would love to have a **seaweed wrap**.

Jerry:　Why would you want to do that?

Diane:　It helps **combat** cellulite. So do **mud packs**.

Jerry:　Women are strange creatures. Well, if you want to go, the **spa** isn't far from here.

Diane:　Great! I would love to get a **foot massage** too.

Jerry:　They do that at spas?

Diane:　Sure do.

Jerry:　Hmm. Well, what are we waiting for?

(傑瑞和黛安在藥局)

傑瑞：妳已經查看過這個架上的每個瓶瓶罐罐了。妳在找什麼啊？

黛安：夏天來了。我想找罐局部用的乳霜來消除我的橘皮組織。

傑瑞：嗯。我可不想聽那些小脂肪囊粒使妳的皮膚凹凹凸凸堆擠在一起
　　　的事！

黛安：傑瑞——你這樣並不是在幫我。

傑瑞：我或許不是，但我媽說不定幫得上忙。她是美療師喔。

黛安：真的嗎？她在美容沙龍工作嗎？我想做海藻裹敷。

傑瑞：為什麼妳會想做那個？

黛安：那有助於消除橘皮組織。敷體泥也可以。

傑瑞：女人真是奇怪的生物。那好，如果妳想去的話，那間水療館離這
　　　兒不遠。

黛安：太棒了！我也很想做個腳底按摩。

傑瑞：水療館也幫人做那個啊？

黛安：當然囉。

傑瑞：嗯，那我們還等什麼呢？

 Words & Phrases

1. topical cream [ˋtɑpɪk͡ ͵krim] *n.*
   針對身體局部使用的乳霜

2. cellulite [ˋsɛljəlaɪt] *n.* 橘皮組織
   （臀腿部位凹凸不平的脂肪組織）

3. sac [sæk] *n.* 生物細胞囊

4. lumpy [ˋlʌmpɪ] *adj.* 成塊隆起的

5. salon [səˋlɑn] *n.* 沙龍

6. seaweed wrap [ˋsi͵wid ͵ræp] *n.*
   （身體）海藻裹敷

7. combat [ˋkɑmbæt] *v.* 與……戰鬥

8. mud pack [ˋmʌd ͵pæk] *n.*
   敷體泥漿；敷面泥

9. spa [spɑ] *n.* 水療美容館

10. foot massage [ˋfut mə͵sɑʒ] *n.*
    腳底按摩

健美會話 2 Walk the Walk

CDI-41

(At the spa)

Jerry: Hey mom. This is Diane. She wanted to check out your **services**.

Diane: Hello, Mrs. Mok. It's nice to meet you.

Mrs. Mok: You too, dear. What can I help you with?

Diane: I wanted to find out what kind of treatments you have.

Mrs. Mok: Here is a list of services. This **package** here is for a **day spa** and it's on sale.

Diane: Wow! **Nail care**, **body massage**, **Dead Sea mud treatment** and **hydrotherapy**.

Jerry: Mom, I don't see any thing for foot massages.

Mrs. Mok: That's under **individual** services. Here it is – **Pedicure**.

Jerry: That's a foot massage?

(Diane winks at Mrs. Mok)

Mrs. Mok: Uh, sure is, honey. Would you like one?

Jerry: Why not.

Diane: And I'll **book** a day spa for tomorrow. Jerry, meet with me afterwards; I want to take a look at your toes.

Jerry: What do mean? Why my toes?

Diane: You'll see!

（在水療館）

傑　瑞：嘿，老媽。這位是黛安。她想看看你們的服務項目。

黛　安：哈囉，莫太太。很高興認識您。

莫太太：我也是，親愛的。我能幫妳做什麼呢？

黛　安：我想知道你們這邊有哪些美療方法。

莫太太：這兒有服務項目列表。這裡這個是日間水療套裝療程，現在正在特惠中。

黛　安：哇！有指甲護理、全身按摩、死海泥護理和水療。

傑　瑞：老媽，我怎麼都沒看到腳底按摩。

莫太太：那是屬於個別服務。在這兒——足部修護。

傑　瑞：那就是腳底按摩？

（黛安對莫太太使個眼色）

莫太太：呃，當然囉，親愛的。你想不想做一次啊？

傑　瑞：有何不可。

黛　安：而我要預約明天來做日間水療。傑瑞，做完之後咱們碰個頭，我想看看你的腳趾。

傑　瑞：什麼意思？為什麼要看我的腳趾？

黛　安：到時候你就知道了！

 Words & Phrases

1. service [ˈsɝvɪs] *n.* 服務

2. package [ˈpækɪdʒ] *n.* 整套
（療程、旅行等）

3. day spa [ˈde ˌspɑ] *n.* 日間水療

4. nail care [ˈnel ˌkɛr] *n.* 指甲護理

5. body massage [ˈbɑdɪ məˌsɑʒ] *n.*
全身按摩

6. Dead Sea mud treatment
[ˈdɛd ˈsi ˈmʌd ˌtritmənt] *n.*
死海泥護理

7. hydrotherapy [ˌhaɪdrəˈθɛrəpɪ] *n.* 水療

8. pedicure [ˈpɛdɪkjʊr] *n.*
修趾甲；足部美容保養

9. book [bʊk] *v.* 預約；預定

活力金句 Pop-up Q&A

也許你會想問…… CDI-42

【如何選擇優質 Spa ?】

你： How do I know if a spa or retreat will offer quality service?
我怎麼知道某個水療或舒壓療程是否能提供優質服務？

美容師： Make sure the facilities are clean, the staff is well trained and the products used are suitable for your skin type.
要確定設備乾淨、員工訓練精良，還有使用的產品適合你的肌膚類型。

【流汗能瘦身嗎？】

你： Can I sweat off pounds by sitting in a sauna?
我能不能就坐在三溫暖烤箱室裡，靠流汗來減輕體重？

美容師： No. You just lose water. Make sure not to use the sauna before working out.
不行。你只會流失掉水份。要確定運動前不要使用三溫暖。

【乾乾的也能做保養？】

你 What is "dry skin brushing"?
什麼叫「乾刷皮膚」？

美容師： When your skin is dry, take a body brush to brush **gently** from your feet and upward. This **removes** the dead **layer** of skin.
在你皮膚是乾的的時候，用身體刷從腳開始向上輕刷你的皮膚。這會清除皮膚死去的舊表層。

■ 也許你會想說……

【不敢去 Spa ……】

你： I'm not going to a spa. My skin is terrible! They will laugh.
我才不去做水療呢。我的皮膚糟透了！他們一定會笑我。

朋友： If they laugh then you are at the wrong spa.
如果他們笑你，那你就選錯水療館了。

【想改善膚質……】

你： I wish I had **glowing** skin like yours.
我希望我像你一樣擁有明亮的肌膚。

朋友： The girls at the spa make my skin like this. Do you want to go with me some time?
水療館的美容師們讓我的皮膚變成這樣。你要不要什麼時候跟我一起去呢？

 Words & Phrases

1. gently [ˋʤɛntlɪ] *adv.* 溫和地

2. remove [rɪˋmuv] *v.* 移除；清除

3. layer [ˋleɚ] *n.* 層

4. glowing [ˋgloɪŋ] *adj.* 閃亮的；明亮的

健美加油站 ⓆⒶ Double Page

🔲 十分鐘肩頸按摩法 DIY Shoulder and Neck Massage

讓專業人士按摩真是舒服極了！但是並不是每個人都有時間和金錢來享受這種奢侈。下面這套簡單的按摩法只需要利用一把直立式的椅子，不用按摩油，衣著隨意，在哪兒都能做。不妨找朋友互相按摩緊繃的肩頸，對舒緩神經、提振精神很有效喔！

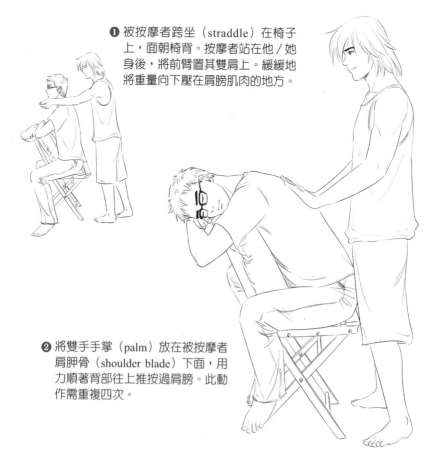

❶ 被按摩者跨坐（straddle）在椅子上，面朝椅背。按摩者站在他／她身後，將前臂置其雙肩上。緩緩地將重量向下壓在肩膀肌肉的地方。

❷ 將雙手手掌（palm）放在被按摩者肩胛骨（shoulder blade）下面，用力順著背部往上推按過肩膀。此動作需重複四次。

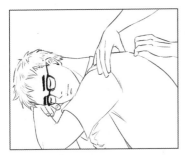

❸ 從頸部下方至手臂上方揉捏（knead）肩膀。

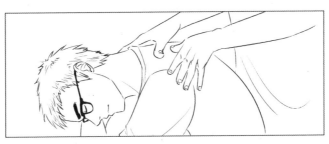

❹ 從下背部開始，將大拇指放在脊椎（spine）兩側。以畫圓圈（circular）移動的方式朝上往頸部按摩。

❺ 用雙手按摩頭部。從頸部往上到額頭、太陽穴（temple），再往下按回頸部。按太陽穴時力道要輕。

❻ 腕部和手部保持放鬆，用手的外側「砍」（chop）肩膀肌肉的部份。一次一邊，動作要快速短促。

❼ 手掌彎成杯狀拍打肩膀。一次一邊。

❽ 用手往下使勁搋（swipe）對方的背部以紓解壓力。之後換另一隻手做。重複五次。

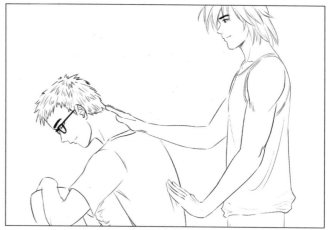

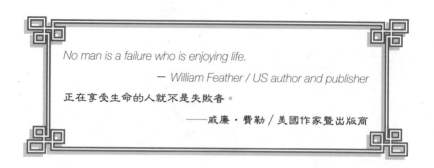

No man is a failure who is enjoying life.

— William Feather / US author and publisher

正在享受生命的人就不是失敗者。

──戚廉‧費勒／美國作家暨出版商

MEMO

Chapter 7

Smell Therapy
神奇的芳香療法

芳香療法並非經科學驗證的醫療方法，但我們

真的需要科學來告訴我們氣味會對我們造成影

響嗎？當我們聞到花香時會微笑，聞到垃圾的

臭味時就會反胃。芳香療法運用具神奇力量的

精油來影響我們的身心。人們選擇使用芳香療

法是因為有個人的體驗，也因為他們相信前人

的體驗。

CDII-01

Aromatherapy is not a scientifically proven method of healing, but does one really need science to tell us smell can affect us? When we smell a flower, we smile. When we smell garbage, our stomach turns. Aromatherapy uses powerful essential oils to influence our body and minds. People choose to use it because of their personal experiences with it, and because they believe the experiences of others before them.

基本行話  The Lingo

CDII-02

❶ aromatherapy [ə͵romə`θɛrəpɪ]	芳香療法 *n.*
❷ incense [`ɪnsɛns]	薰香；（祭拜時用的）香 *n.*
❸ scent [sɛnt]	香味 *n.*
❹ essential oil [ɪ`sɛnʃəl `ɔɪl]	精油 *n.*
❺ blend [blɛnd]	混合 *v.*
❻ healing effect [`hilɪŋ ɪ`fɛkt]	療效 *n.*
❼ synergy [`sɪnədʒɪ]	複合作用；複方（精油）*n.*
❽ oil burner [`ɔɪl ͵bɜnə]	薰香台；薰香燈 *n.*
❾ dilute [dɪ`lut]	稀釋 *v.*
❿ carrier oil [`kærɪə ͵ɔɪl]	基礎油 *n.*

暖身練習 Word Workout

CDII-03

A: **Aromatherapy** is getting more and more popular.
B: That's true. Sometimes I will also burn **incense** to help me relax.

A: 芳香療法越來越流行了。
B: 的確是。有時我也會點薰香幫助自己放鬆。

A: I like the scents of a few different **essential oils**. How do I choose?
B: Using a guide, choose a few and **blend** together oils that complement each other.

A: 我喜歡幾種不同精油的香味。我要怎麼選擇呢？
B: 使用指南，選幾種精油然後把可以互補的精油混合在一起。

A: Is it true that blending too many oils can negate their **healing effects**?
B: That's right. You have to mix correct amounts of a few selected oils to create **synergy**.

A: 混合太多種精油真的會消滅它們的療效嗎？
B: 沒錯。你必須以正確的劑量混合幾種特選的精油才能製造出複方精油。

A: For healing benefits, I like to burn essential oils in an oil burner.
B: I prefer to **dilute** them with **carrier oil** and use as massage oil.

A: 為了得到療效，我喜歡用薰香台點精油。
B: 我比較喜歡把精油用基礎油稀釋，當作按摩油來使用。

健美會話 1　　Talk the Talk

(Diane and Alan are out for an evening walk.)

Alan: **Yummy**. The smell of chocolate coming from that dessert place is making me hungry.

Diane: Me too. Let's go in for some cake and coffee.

Alan: No coffee for me. I've **had trouble sleeping** lately.

Diane: Really? Are you **stressed out** about something?

Alan: I have a lot of **pressure** from work right now.

Diane: Losing sleep won't help you. Have you tried having a **relaxing** bath with **lavender** oil before going to bed?

Alan: Aromatherapy doesn't work.

Diane: It does for me.

Alan: Smells can't influence how you feel.

Diane: How do you explain suddenly feeling hungry when you passed that dessert shop?

Alan: Well ... uh ... I ah ...

Diane: That's what I thought.

（黛安和艾倫傍晚出門散步）

艾倫：好香啊。那家甜點舖飄來的巧克力香讓我覺得餓了。

黛安：我也是。咱們進店裡去來點蛋糕和咖啡吧。

艾倫：我不要咖啡。我最近一直睡得不好。

黛安：真的啊？你是為了什麼而有壓力嗎？

艾倫：我現在工作壓力很大。

黛安：失眠可幫不了你。你有沒有試過睡前泡個令人放鬆的薰衣草精油浴？

艾倫：芳香療法沒有用啦。

黛安：對我就有用。

艾倫：氣味又不會影響你的感覺。

黛安：那你經過那家點心舖的時候突然覺得餓了，你做何解釋？

艾倫：這個嘛……呃……我……

黛安：我就是我的想法。

 Words & Phrases

1. yummy [ˈjʌmɪ] *adj.* 可口的

2. have trouble doing sth. 做某事有困擾

3. stress out 感到壓力

4. pressure [ˈprɛʃ.ər] *n.* 壓力

5. relaxing [rɪˈlæksɪŋ] *adj.* 令人放鬆的

6. lavender [ˈlævəndə] *n.* 薰衣草

健美會話2  Walk the Walk

 CDII-05

(The next day. Diane calls up Alan.)

Diane: Did you use any of the essential oils I gave you last night?

Alan: Yeah, I did.

Diane: What ones?

Alan: Well, I was feeling cold so I blended **ginger**, **patchouli** and **frankincense** with carrier oil, and then massaged my feet.

Diane: Great.

Alan: To relax I had a lavender bath and burned **ylang-ylang** in an oil burner.

Diane: Wow! **I bet** you were really relaxed.

Alan: I was. However I got so excited by how relaxed I felt that I grabbed the peppermint and rushed over to my neighbor who had a **stomachache**.

Diane: That was nice of you. Then did you go to bed?

Alan: No. We **stayed up** for hours researching aromatherapy on the Internet. I'm totally **exhausted**.

Diane: Well, you're on your own on that one, Alan. There aren't any essential oils that can cure **curiosity**!

（隔天黛安打電話給艾倫）

黛安：你昨晚有沒有用我給你的那些精油？

艾倫：有，我用了。

黛安：用了哪些？

艾倫：我昨天覺得冷冷的，所以就把薑、廣藿香還有乳香和基礎油混合在一塊兒，然後用來按摩雙腳。

黛安：很好。

艾倫：為了達到放鬆的效果，我泡了個薰衣草浴，還用薰香台點依蘭精油。

黛安：哇！你一定真的很放鬆。

艾倫：我是很放鬆。可是我因為感到那麼放鬆了而興奮，所以一把抓起薄荷油就跑去找胃痛的鄰居。

黛安：你人真好。之後你有沒有去睡覺？

艾倫：沒有。我們熬夜好幾個小時，上網搜尋芳香療法。真是把我累壞了。

黛安：嗯，這你就得自己想辦法了，艾倫。沒有任何精油能治好奇心哦！

 Words & Phrases

1. ginger [ˋdʒɪndʒɚ] n. 薑

2. patchouli [pæˋtʃulɪ] n. 廣藿香

3. frankincense [ˋfræŋkɪnˌsɛns] n. 乳香

4. ylang-ylang [ˋliŋˋliŋ] n. 依蘭依蘭（精油）

5. I bet ... 我確定……

6. peppermint [ˋpɛpɚˌmɪnt] n. 薄荷油

7. stomachache [ˋstʌməkˌek] n. 胃痛

8. stay up 熬夜

9. exhausted [ɪgˋzɔstɪd] adj. 疲憊的；筋疲力盡的

10. curiosity [ˌkjʊrɪˋɑsətɪ] n. 好奇心

活力金句 Pop-up Q&A

■ 也許你會想問……

【精油不會有問題嗎？】

你： Are all oils safe for everyone?
精油對每個人都安全嗎？

專家： No. Some people may experience reactions such as **reddening** of the skin or **itchiness**.
不是。有人或許會發生例如皮膚紅腫或發癢的反應。

【我適合用精油嗎？】

你： What can I do to make sure an oil is safe for me?
我要怎麼才能確定某種精油對我?對安全？

專家： Always consult a trained aroma **therapist** before using an oil.
在使用精油之前，一定要請教受過訓練的芳香療法專家。

【精油越純越好？】

你： Do I always have to dilute essential oils?
我一定總是得稀釋精油嗎？

專家： Almost always. The general rule is to dilute oils unless you are **instructed** to use them **neat**.
幾乎是。一般的原則是精油都要加以稀釋，除非有人指示你要使用純的。

■ 也許你會想說……

【對療效有點存疑】

你： I am a little **hesitant** about using **alternative therapies**.
我對於使用另類療法有點遲疑。

朋友： It's always **scary** trying something new. But you might just find something that works for you.
嘗試新事物總是令人膽怯的。但你或許會找到對你有用的療法。

【好像什麼都不懂……】

你： I feel stupid asking so many questions.
我覺得問這麼多問題很蠢。

朋友： I'll go with you and we can ask questions together.
我陪你去，我們可以一起問。

Words & Phrases

1. redden [ˋrɛdn̩] *v.* 使發紅

2. itchiness [ˋɪtʃɪnəs] *n.* 發癢

3. therapist [ˋθɛrəpɪst] *n.* 治療學家

4. instruct [ɪnˋstrʌkt] *v.* 指示

5. neat [nit] *adj.* 純的；整潔的；
【口】很好的

6. hesitant [ˋhɛzətənt] *adj.* 遲疑的

7. alternative [ɔlˋtɜnətɪv] *adj.* 另類的；
可替代另一個的

8. therapy [ˋθɛrəpɪ] *n.* 療法

9. scary [ˋskɛrɪ] *adj.* 嚇人的；可怕的

健美加油站 Inspiration Lounge

■ 芳香療法的歷史 The History of Aromatherapy

芳香療法指的是運用從植物中萃取（retrieve）的精油來改變身體及情緒狀態。運用植物治療功效的歷史悠久，早在西元前七千年，人類就利用植物香料結合橄欖油（olive oil）和芝麻油（sesame oil）來製造膏藥（ointment）。然而，芳香療法這個詞一直到一九二〇年才由一位名叫雷內・蓋特佛賽的人所創造。

■ 精油的保存 Take Care of Essential Oils

精油是容易揮發（volatile）的物質，需要悉心照顧才能長時間保存。精油可吸入體內或經由按摩、泡澡讓肌膚吸收。它們必須儲放在陰涼的地方。購買時以少量為原則。如果要用基礎油稀釋，只要稀釋二至四個月內使用的份量即可。未經稀釋的精油如果妥善保存，存放期限可以長達數年。好好呵護它們，它們就會好好呵護你。

■ 讓精油照顧你 Let Essentials Oils Take Care of You

CDII-07

不同的精油可以達到不同的效果，有些具有抗病毒（antiviral）、抗菌（anti-bacterial）、防腐（antiseptic）、提高免疫力（immunity-boosting）及止痛（pain-killing）的功能。有些精油是用來鎮定及放鬆情緒，其他則有些可以提振思緒並活化腦力。認識以下這些精油，看看哪些對你有用吧！

- 佛手柑 Bergamot [ˋbɝɡəˌmɑt]
  - 能防止發炎（inflammation），抑制細菌滋長。可舒緩哀傷、憂鬱、焦慮（anxiety），並刺激消化（digestion）。
  - 適合調配的精油：天竺葵、薰衣草、橙花、檀香（sandalwood）、依蘭依蘭。

- 甘菊 Chamomile [ˋkæməˌmaɪl]
  - 舒緩壓力的極佳良方，也適合乾燥敏感（sensitive）的肌膚。
  - 適合調配的精油：薰衣草、花梨木（rosewood）、檀香。

- 天竺葵 Geranium [dʒɜˋrenɪəm]
  - 可提振精神，活化血液並增強體力。
  - 適合調配的精油：橙花、玫瑰、佛手柑、薰衣草和檀香。

- 薰衣草 Lavender [ˋlævəndə]
  - 可舒緩頭痛，抗憂鬱（antidepressant），並有助於修護（regenerate）受損肌

膚及消炎鎮定。
- 適合調配的精油：佛手柑、天竺葵、花梨木、玫瑰草（palmarosa）和檀香。

● 檸檬 Lemon [ˈlɛmən]
- 有助於澄清思慮，促進循環（circulation），是強效的防腐劑。
- 適合調配的精油：任何柑橘類（citrus）精油、佛手柑、玫瑰精油（rose otto）和依蘭依蘭

● 橙花 Neroli [ˈnɛrəlɪ]
- 可用於消除伸展紋（stretch mark）和疤痕（scar），提高免疫力，消除鼻塞（decongestant），紓解壓力。
- 適合調配的精油：佛手柑、薰衣草、檀香、天竺葵和依蘭依蘭。

● 薄荷 Peppermint [ˈpɛpəˌmɪnt]
- 適用於胃部不適，並能使全身舒暢充滿活力。
- 適合調配的精油：檸檬、尤加利（eucalyptus）、迷迭香、茶樹（tea tree）和天竺葵。

● 玫瑰 Rose [roz]
- 可改善生理（menstrual）和更年期症狀（menopausal complaints）、睡眠問題、胃部不適，及多種皮膚疾病。
- 適合調配的精油：橙花、檀香、薰衣草、乳香（frankincense）和天竺葵。

● 迷迭香 Rosemary [ˈrozˌmɛrɪ]
- 可幫助消化、抗憂鬱，並可提神及刺激循環。
- 適合的調配成分：柑橘類精油。

● 依蘭依蘭 Ylang-ylang [ˈliŋˈliŋ]
- 極適用於增添性感魅力和放鬆，並有助於平衡激動的情緒。
- 適合調配的精油：柑橘及清淡的花香（floral）精油、天竺葵、薰衣草、絲柏（cypress）和玫瑰草。

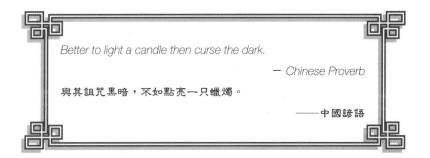

Better to light a candle then curse the dark.

— *Chinese Proverb*

與其詛咒黑暗，不如點亮一只蠟燭。

——中國諺語

Chapter 8

Healthy Space
美化環境有益健康

健康的環境和友善的面孔就像飲食和運動一樣，對擁有健康的生活而言很重要。要活出有意義的圓滿人生，事物、地方和人都扮演著重要的角色。家是我們的庇護所，而朋友、家人則是我們的支援系統。這些事物都會影響並塑造我們日常的感受與認知。

 CDII-08

Healthy spaces and friendly faces are as important to healthy living as diet and exercise. Things, places and people play an important role in living a rewarding and full life. Homes are our place of refuge and friends and family are our support systems. These are the things that influence and shape our daily perceptions.

基本行話 The Lingo

CDII-09

❶ organize [ˈɔrgəˌnaɪz]	組織；規劃；使有條理 v.
❷ environment [ɪnˈvaɪrənmənt]	環境 n.
❸ well-being [ˈwɛlˈbiɪŋ]	健康；幸福 n.
❹ relationship [rɪˈleʃənˌʃɪp]	關係 n.
❺ habit [ˈhæbɪt]	習慣 n.
❻ addict [əˈdɪkt]	沉溺；上癮 v.
❼ cut out	戒除
❽ inspiring [ɪnˈspaɪrɪŋ]	鼓舞的；有啓發性的 adj.
❾ hobby [ˈhɑbɪ]	嗜好 n.
❿ motivate [ˈmotəˌvet]	激發；給……動機 v.

暖身練習 Word Workout

CDII-10

A: Why do you spend so much time **organizing** everything?
B: A clean and organized **environment** is important to my **well-being**.

A: 你為什麼要花那麼多時間打點每件事情呢？
B: 一個乾淨又有條理的環境對我的健康幸福很重要。

A: I have an unhealthy **relationship** with coffee.
B: Yes, drinking too much coffee is a bad **habit**.

A: 我太依賴咖啡了。
B: 是的，喝太多咖啡是個壞習慣。

A: I'm totally **addicted** to chocolate. Let's go buy some.
B: None for me. I'm trying to **cut out** chocolate from my diet.

A: 我對巧克力完全上癮了。我們去買一些吧。
B: 我一點都不要。我正試著把巧克力從我的飲食中戒除。

A: I find it **inspiring** that you have so many **hobbies**.
B: It sometimes feels like I have too many. It's hard to stay **motivated** to do them.

A: 你有那麼多嗜好，我覺得蠻具啟發性的。
B: 有時候我覺得我的嗜好太多了。要保持動力從事那麼多活動很難。

  Talk the Talk

 CDII-11

(Alan, Diane and Jerry are out for lunch.)

Diane: Jerry, the reason we asked you for lunch is that we want to talk to you about your **lifestyle**.

Alan: We love and **support** you, but we think you could use a few **adjustments** in the way you live.

Jerry: I make changes. Just yesterday I tried a different brand of beer.

Diane: That is exactly what we are talking about. You never take anything seriously.

Alan: She's right. You have a list of bad habits a mile long. Your only hobby is watching TV and your house is gross.

Jerry: My house is gross?

Diane: Really gross. It's **smelly**, dirty and totally unorganized. It also wouldn't hurt to get a plant. Living things are good in a home.

Jerry: I have a plant. It's on the table right beside my couch.

Diane: That's called **mold**, Jerry.

（艾倫、黛安和傑瑞到外面吃午餐）

黛安：傑瑞，我們之所以找你吃午餐，是因為我們想和你聊聊你的生活
　　　方式。

艾倫：我們愛你，也支持你，但是我們認為你的生活方式或許可以做些
　　　調整。

傑瑞：我有做改變啊。就在昨天，我試喝了一種不同牌子的啤酒。

黛安：我們就是在說這個。你對任何事情都不正經。

艾倫：她說的對。你的壞習慣列成清單肯定又臭又長。你唯一的嗜好就
　　　是看電視，而你的房子噁心死了。

傑瑞：我的房子噁心？

黛安：真的很噁心。你的房子有臭味，又髒，而且一團亂。弄個植物擺
　　　擺也無傷呀。家裡放些有生命的東西很不錯。

傑瑞：我有植物啊。就在我沙發旁邊的桌上。

黛安：那玩意兒叫作黴菌，傑瑞。

Words & Phrases

1. lifestyle [ˋlaɪfˏstaɪl] *n.* 生活方式

2. support [səˋport] *v.* 支持

3. adjustment [əˋdʒʌstmənt] *n.* 調整

4. smelly [ˋsmɛlɪ] *adj.* 有臭味的

5. mold [mold] *n.* 黴菌

健美會話2　　Walk the Walk

CDII-12

(One hour later)

Jerry:　OK! I got it already! Stop your **nagging**.

Diane:　We don't want to overwhelm you. You can start with some **minor** changes.

Alan:　Like **cutting down** on beer, watching less TV and buying a **vacuum**.

Jerry:　*(Gasping)* I can't breathe.

Diane:　They say home is where the heart is, so we should start there.

Alan:　Your living space is very important. Diane and I can come over and help you houseclean.

Jerry:　This is all happening a little fast. Are all of these changes necessary?

Diane:　You know better than us. Are you happy?

Jerry:　Well, I have been feeling a little **sluggish** these past few years and I do seem to have lost a little of my sex **appeal**.

Diane:　I have two words for you, sexy man — energy and confidence. Develop those qualities, and the ladies will be knocking down your door.

Jerry:　Well, if I am expecting ladies we should start with cleaning the bedroom!

(一個小時之後)

傑瑞：好啦！我已經了解了！別再嘮叨了。

黛安：我們並不想讓你受不了。你可以從小小的改變開始做起。

艾倫：像是少喝點啤酒，少看電視，再買台吸塵器。

傑瑞：（倒抽一口氣）我不能呼吸了。

黛安：俗話說「家是心之所在」，所以我們就從家開始吧。

艾倫：你的起居空間非常重要。黛安和我可以過去幫你打掃屋子。

傑瑞：這一切發生得太快了點。這些改變都是必要的嗎？

黛安：你比我們更清楚。你快樂嗎？

傑瑞：嗯，我過去這些年來是覺得有點懶，而且確實好像喪失了一點我
　　　的性感魅力。

黛安：性感帥哥，我送你兩個字詞——活力和自信。發揮這兩種特質，
　　　美眉就會蜂擁而至把你的門都給拆了。

傑瑞：唔，如果我在等美眉上門，那我們就應該從打掃臥室開始！

 Words & Phrases

1. nag [næg] *v.* 嘮叨

2. minor [ˋmaɪnɚ] *adj.* 較小的；次要的

3. cut down 減少

4. vacuum [ˋvækjuəm] *n.* 真空吸塵器
   (= vacuum cleaner)

5. houseclean [ˋhaʊs͵klin] *v.* 打掃房屋

6. sluggish [ˋslʌgɪʃ] *a.* 懶散的

7. appeal [əˋpil] *n.* 吸引力

8. knock down 拆毀

活力金句 ❓🅰 Pop-up Q&A

也許你會想問……

CDII-13

【在辦公室容易累？】

你： Why do **air-conditioned** rooms cause me to feel tired?
為什麼有空調的房間會讓我覺得累？

專家： **Atmospheres** that have low **humidity** levels cause **fatigue**.
Try placing a bowl of water in the room.
濕度低的空氣會引起疲勞。試試在房間內放碗水。

【植物有什麼用？】

你： Why is it good to have plants at work and in your home?
為什麼在辦公室和家裡放置植物很好？

專家： Plants help break down **radiation** that comes from your
TV and computer.
植物有助於破壞電視和電腦產生的輻射線。

【燈光有影響嗎？】

你： Why do **fluorescent lights** make me feel **lethargic**?
為什麼日光燈會讓我昏昏欲睡？

專家： Try changing the lights to **full spectrum bulbs** or get out-
side for a walk during the lunch hour.
試試將燈換成全光譜燈泡，或是在午餐時間出去走一走。

■ 也許你會想說……

【別說自己笨】

你： I am so stupid! I can't do anything right!
我真笨！什麼事都做不好！

朋友： You are not stupid; you just find this difficult. You can do many things well.
你不笨，你只是覺得這個比較難。你可以做好很多事的。

【辛苦了！】

你： I'm exhausted. I stayed up so late trying to get this project finished.
我累壞了。我熬夜到很晚，才把這個企劃案完成。

朋友： You did a great job on it. You must feel very satisfied.
你企劃案做得很棒。你一定覺得很滿意。

 Words & Phrases

1. air-conditioned [ˈɛr.kən.dɪʃənd] *adj.*
   有空調的

2. atmosphere [ˈætməs.fɪr] *n.*
   空氣；氣氛

3. humidity [hjuˈmɪdətɪ] *n.* 溼度

4. fatigue [fəˈtig] *n.* 疲勞；倦怠

5. radiation [.redɪˈeʃən] *n.* 輻射

6. fluorescent light [.fluəˈrɛsn̩t ˈlaɪt]
   n. 日光燈

7. lethargic [lɪˈθɑrdʒɪk] *adj.*
   嗜睡的；昏昏欲睡的

8. full spectrum bulb
   [ˈfʊl ˈspɛktrəm .bʌlb]
   n. 全光譜燈泡

健美加油站 Q A Inspiration Lounge

■ 漣漪效應 The Ripple Effect

石頭落水時會產生漣漪。同樣地，積極的（positive）和消極的（negative）舉動也會在人與人之間產生漣漪效應。這些舉動會影響我們對世界和對自己的觀感。積極的生活不是要鼓吹理想、貶低他人的價值或揮霍放縱人生，而是要開闊心胸（open-mindedness）、抱持疑問、分享想法並鼓勵他人。無論在家、職場或街上，成功圓滿的生活就是要對自己的行動用心。一個人的世界觀和自我形象（self-image）都會微妙地受到父母、朋友和社會的影響。人人都有製造正面或負面結果的力量。負起影響他人態度的責任吧！你將會得到正面的回饋。

■ 全力以赴 Doing the Best We Can

我們盡自己所能創造一個溫暖的家、過好日子，即使不如意還是要面帶微笑。有時我們會因生活繁重，而需要一些額外的幫助，但千萬別被那些搞得你團團轉的事情打倒！勇敢地站起來大聲說：「我可以做得更好！」

要改變生活方式，需要一些力量和技巧。以下是能幫助你充電增加能量的一些方法。

■ 充電十招 10 Ways to Recharge

1. 和消極的人在一起會讓人覺得很糟。別把寶貴精力浪費在老想著「這杯子已經空了一半」（the glass is half empty）那種人身上。讓自己身邊圍繞著快樂、有信心又積極的人，你會發現生命輕鬆、有趣多了。

2. 到大自然中走走吧！到海邊、鄉間或山上會讓你覺得身心舒暢。新鮮的空氣中充滿負離子（negative ion），會增加血液中的氧氣（oxygen），給你滿滿的活力。

3. 試著維持固定的（consistent）睡眠和用餐時間。這有助於讓你的身

體狀態保持規律（rhythm）。生活紊亂絕對是耗損能量的殺手（energy zapper）。

4. 快而淺的呼吸會消耗能量。最佳的呼吸法是要像嬰兒一樣，以緩慢的深呼吸將氣吸入你的腹部（abdomen）。

5. 工作時無法保持清醒嗎？把鞋子脫掉，把雙腳釋放出來。動動你的腳趾，轉轉你的腳踝，稍微按摩一下雙腳。從腳後跟開始，以畫圓圈的動作往前按到你的腳趾部分。

6. 試著避免在深夜做運動。這樣會加速你的血液循環，讓你難以入睡。好好睡一覺，第二天早上再做運動。

7. 整個禮拜都沒空上健身房？沒關係，但是別試圖在週末彌補過來。突然從事激烈的運動會掏空你全身的精力喔！

8. 累了嗎？那就喝水吧。脫水會導致頭痛、疲倦和眼睛酸痛等症狀（symptom）。大口喝（gulp）個一、二杯水，你會馬上恢復活力。

9. 吃完午餐之後，很想倒頭趴在桌上嗎？不如出去散步個十分鐘。研究顯示這樣可以提升精力達兩小時之久。

10. 找點有趣的事來做！無聊是能量的頭號殺手之一。做你喜歡做的事，讓你的身心持續受激勵。

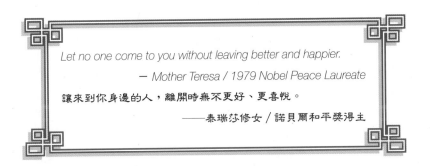

Let no one come to you without leaving better and happier.

— Mother Teresa / 1979 Nobel Peace Laureate

讓來到你身邊的人，離開時無不更好、更喜悅。

——泰瑞莎修女／諾貝爾和平獎得主

Section Three

You Are What You Eat
均衡飲食

3

Chapter 9

Eating for Health
吃出美味與健康

我們活在一個資訊時代。每一天，電視、雜誌、看板和網路都在告訴我們該吃什麼。食品標示則告訴我們哪些食物是低脂、高脂、無脂及富含飽和脂肪。感激不盡！但是這一大堆詞彙到底是什麼意思呢？有選擇性很棒，但多到我們無法招架就另當別論了。身為一位現代的消費者蠻累人的，但是只要掌握一些事實，你就可以控制該或不該讓身體攝取某些東西。

CDII-14

We live in an information age. Each day TV, magazines, billboards and the Internet tell us what we should eat. Food labels inform us which foods are low fat, high fat, no fat and full of saturated fat. Thanks! But what does it all mean? Choice is great until we feel overwhelmed. Being a modern consumer can be exhausting, but with a few facts you can take control over what you put and don't put into your body.

 基本行話 The Lingo

CDII-15

❶ food pyramid [ˈfud ˌpɪrəmɪd]	食物金字塔 *n.*
❷ serving [ˈsɜvɪŋ]	一份；每餐份 *n.*
❸ whole grain [ˈhol ˌgren]	全穀類 *n.*
❹ enriched [ɪnˈrɪtʃt]	增進營養的；營養強化的 *adj.*
❺ nutrition [njuˈtrɪʃən]	營養 *n.*
❻ synthetic [sɪnˈθɛtɪk]	合成的；人造的 *adj.*
❼ nutrient [ˈnjutrɪənt]	營養物 *n.*
❽ refine [rɪˈfaɪn]	精煉；精製 *v.*
❾ low-fat [ˈloˈfæt]	低脂的 *adj.*
❿ skim milk [ˈskim ˈmɪlk]	脫脂牛奶 *n.*

暖身練習 Word Workout

A: This **food pyramid** stresses daily **servings** of **whole grain** food.
B: That's good. Grains are the foundation of good **nutrition**.

A: 這個食物金字塔強調每日所需的全穀類食品。
B: 那很好。穀類是營養好的基礎。

A: What does "**enriched**" mean?
B: It means that **synthetic nutrients** have been added to replace the nutrients that were destroyed in the **refining** process.

A: 「營養強化」是什麼意思？
B: 那是指添加人工合成營養物質，來代替在精製過程中被破壞的營養成份。

A: What are you going to have, the hamburger or grilled chicken?
B: Chicken. I'm on a **low-fat** diet so I am only eating lean meats.

A: 你要吃什麼？漢堡還是烤雞？
B: 我要雞肉。我現在要吃低脂餐，所以只吃瘦肉。

A: Do you want some cream in your coffee?
B: I would prefer **skim milk** if you have any.

A: 你的咖啡要加奶精嗎？
B: 如果你有的話，我想加脫脂牛奶。

 健美會話1 Talk the Talk

CDII-17

(Alan and Diane are at the library.)

Alan: What are you writing about? You have been **scribbling** down notes for an hour.

Diane: I'm copying out information on **dietary guidelines**.

Alan: I rarely notice what I eat. Modern **civilization** has made it so easy to eat out all the time.

Diane: Learning a little about food might help you to cross the **plateau** you reached in your workouts.

Alan: What do you mean?

Diane: If your diet is too **high in fats** then it really doesn't matter how hard you work out. You will stay the same weight.

Alan: Maybe, but I think it's all just **mumbo jumbo**. For example, it says to eat 6 to 11 servings of grains and **cereals** a day. Who sits down and has 6 to 11 **meals** a day?

Diane: A serving doesn't **equal** a meal! One **slice** of bread equals a serving. Eat a sandwich and that's two servings.

Alan: Maybe I should hire you to be my **dietician**!

（艾倫和黛安在圖書館）

艾倫：妳在寫什麼啊？妳已經東抄西抄寫了一個小時了。

黛安：我在抄飲食指南的資訊。

艾倫：我很少注意自己吃什麼。現代文明已經使得一天到晚外食變得輕鬆簡單了。

黛安：了解食物一點或許能幫你跨越運動上碰到的停滯期。

艾倫：什麼意思？

黛安：如果你的飲食脂肪含量過高，那麼你多努力運動都沒用。你還是會維持一樣的體重。

艾倫：或許吧，可是我認為那只不過都亂講的。舉例來說好了，飲食指南上說一天要吃六到十一份的穀類或穀類製品。誰會在一天之內坐下來吃六到十一餐呢？

黛安：一個食份不等於一餐！一片麵包就相當於一份。吃個三明治就是兩份。

艾倫：或許我應該聘請妳來當我的營養師！

 Words & Phrases

1. scribble [ˋskrɪbl̩] v. 亂寫；塗鴉

2. dietary [ˋdaɪəˌtɛrɪ] adj. 飲食的

3. guideline [ˋgaɪdˌlaɪn] n. 指南

4. civilization [ˌsɪvl̩əˋzeʃən] n. 文明

5. plateau [plæˋto] n. 高原；
   （學習等的）停滯期

6. high in fat 脂肪含量高

7. mumbo jumbo [ˋmʌmbo ˋjʌmbo]
   n. 胡言亂語

8. cereal [ˋsɪrɪəl] n. 穀類；穀類食品

9. meal [mil] n. 一餐

10. equal [ˋikwəl] v. 等於；相當於

11. slice [slaɪs] n. 一片

12. dietician [ˌdaɪəˋtɪʃən] n. 營養師

健美會話2　Walk the Walk

CDII-18

(Alan begins to become interested in his diet.)

Diane: Wow! You are checking out a lot of books. What are you getting?

Alan: This is called *Fun with **Food Groups*** and this one is ***Cholesterol** is Not Your Friend.*

Diane: I see I **sparked** your interest.

Alan: I've always been curious. I just didn't know where to begin.

Diane: It looks like you're off to a good start.

Alan: Did you know that there are 5 food groups?

Diane: Actually I ...

Alan: And the number of calories you need are different than what I need.

Diane: Oh, really?

Alan: I am a super-active man so I need about 2,800 calories a day. And a **sedentary** woman only needs about 1,600 calories a day.

Diane: Hey, watch it!

Alan: Just kidding! You are a very active woman so you should take in 2,200 calories a day.

Diane: Great. I'm well under **quota**. Let's go for cheesecake!

（艾倫開始對他的飲食產生興趣）

黛安：哇！你在看好多書啊。你借了些什麼書啊？

艾倫：這本叫作「食物群樂無窮」，而這一本是「膽固醇不是你的朋友」。

黛安：我看我激發你的興趣了。

艾倫：我一直都很好奇，只是不知道要從何開始。

黛安：看起來你已經有了好的開始。

艾倫：妳知道有五大類食物群嗎？

黛安：其實我……

艾倫：還有，妳需要的卡路里數和我需要的不一樣。

黛安：哦，真的嗎？

艾倫：我是個活動量超大的男生，所以我一天需要兩千八百卡。而老是坐著不動的女生一天只需大約一千六百卡。

黛安：嘿，說話小心點！

艾倫：開玩笑的啦！妳是個很好動的女生，所以妳一天應該攝取兩千兩百卡。

黛安：太好了。我離定量還很遠。咱們去吃乳酪蛋糕吧！

Words & Phrases

1. food group [ˈfud ˌgrup] *n.* 食物群

2. cholesterol [kəˈlɛstəˌrol] *n.* 膽固醇

3. spark [spɑrk] *v.* 引起；點燃；刺激

4. active [ˈæktɪv] *adj.* 活動的；活躍的

5. sedentary [ˈsɛdn̩ˌtɛrɪ] *adj.* 常坐著的；少動的

6. quota [ˈkwotə] *n.* 定量；配額

活力金句 Pop-up Q&A

■ 也許你會想問……

CDII-19

【飲食文化不同怎麼辦？】

你： Is the USDA Food Guide Pyramid the only one in the world?

美國農業部的食物指南金字塔是世上唯一的一個嗎？

營養師： No. There are different food pyramids designed for a variety of cultural diets.

不是。有為各種飲食文化所設計的不同食物金字塔。

【精製不好嗎？】

你： What's wrong with **refined** flour?

精製麵粉有什麼不對的？

營養師： Certain items are **removed** from the wheat, such as wheat **germ**. It means less nutrition for you.

有些物質從小麥中被移除了，例如小麥胚芽。這表示給你的營養較少。

【八杯水的功能是什麼？】

你： Why do I need to drink eight glasses of water every day?

什麼我每天需要喝八杯水？

營養師： We need to drink about 2000cc of water to **replenish** the lost water every day.

我們每天需要喝大約兩千西西的水來補充流失的水份。

■ 也許你會想說……

【不知道怎麼吃……】

你：　I never can **figure out** what I should or shouldn't eat.
　　　我從來就搞不懂應該吃什麼，或不應該吃什麼。

朋友：Perhaps you should ask the health professional to help
　　　you **customize** a diet plan.
　　　也許你應該請健康專家幫你量身打造出一套飲食計劃。

【就是想吃……】

你：　I have changed my diet but I can't stop **craving** foods that
　　　I shouldn't be eating!
　　　我已經改變了飲食習慣，可是無法停止渴望想吃不該吃的食
　　　物！

朋友：You're doing great. Just do your best and don't **be too**
　　　hard on yourself.
　　　你做得很好。盡力就好，不用對自己太嚴苛。

 Words & Phrases

1. refined [rɪ`faɪnd] *adj.* 精製過的

2. item [`aɪtəm] *n.* 項目

3. remove [rɪ`muv] *v.* 移除

4. germ [dʒɝm] *n.* 胚；幼芽

5. replenish [rɪ`plɛnɪʃ] *v.* 補充；斟滿

6. figure [`fɪgjə] out　理解；想出

7. customize [`kʌstə‚maɪz] *v.* 訂製；訂做

8. crave [krev] *v.* 渴望

9. be (too) hard on
　　（過度）嚴苛對待……

119

健美加油站 Inspiration Lounge

■ 健康食物精選 Healthy Food Selection

不同的食物所含的營養也各有不同。多了解食物，針對身體狀況調整飲食，讓你不只吃得飽，還能越吃越健康！

● **富含基礎營養 Super Foods**
為了造就更健康的你，試著在你的飲食中加入莓果（berries）、香蕉、花椰菜（broccoli）、胡蘿蔔、菠菜（spinach）、大蒜（garlic）、油魚（oily fish）、豆類和扁豆（lentils）、堅果和種籽類、酸乳酪、大豆和豆腐。

● **增進能量 Energy Foods**
要提振精力就吃這些食物：香蕉、蜂蜜、木瓜、菠菜、堅果、甜椒（pepper）、甘藷和山藥（yam）。

● **降低癌症風險 Lower the Risk of Cancer**
以下這些食物含有抗癌成分：香蕉、豆類和扁豆、花椰菜、燕麥（oat）、甘藍菜（cabbage）、油魚、木瓜、芒果、種籽類、豆腐、甜椒、菠菜、甘藷和番茄。

● **保護眼睛 A Sight for Sore Eyes**
有助於對抗眼部疾病及鞏固眼睛的食物有：胡蘿蔔、菠菜和葵花籽（sunflower seeds）。

● **舒緩生理期症狀 PMS and Menstrual Problems**
吃吃以下這些食物，可告別生理痛（cramp）和情緒不穩：香蕉、豆類和扁豆、莓果、胡蘿蔔、堅果、油魚、馬鈴薯、山藥、大豆和豆腐。

● **平撫鬱悶情緒 I Feel Sad**
吃香蕉、花椰菜和燕麥有助於解除焦慮和鬱悶的感覺。

■ 維他命 B 提神果汁 B-Vitamin Smoothy

覺得慵懶無力嗎？這兒有個保證提升活力的妙方！將下列材料全放進果汁機內，攪拌至均勻滑順即可。喝下去保證讓你恢復活力！

鳳梨汁（pineapple juice）	125 毫升
純豆奶（plain soymilk）	50 毫升
剝皮切碎的鳳梨 （chopped peeled pineapple）	25 毫升
剝皮、去核切碎的杏桃 （chopped, peeled and pitted apricots）	50 毫升
熟香蕉（ripe banana）	1 根
小麥胚芽（wheat germ）	15 毫升
亞麻子（flax seeds）	10 毫升
魚肝油或大麻油（cod liver or hemp oil）	5 毫升

The future belongs to those who believe in the beauty of

their dreams.

— Eleanor Roosevelt / former First Lady of USA

未來是屬於那些相信自己的夢想是美好的人。

——埃莉諾・羅斯福／前美國總統夫人

Chapter 10

Power Me Up!

補充營養元氣滿點

吃充滿美味天然食品的飲食，當然是得到身體所需各種重要維生素和礦物質較好的方法。然而，在現今這個時代中，我們有很多藉口來解釋？什麼不吃應該吃的食物。如果你決定要猛塞營養補給品，切記要做好研究。營養補給品是藥品，必須被當成藥物看待。

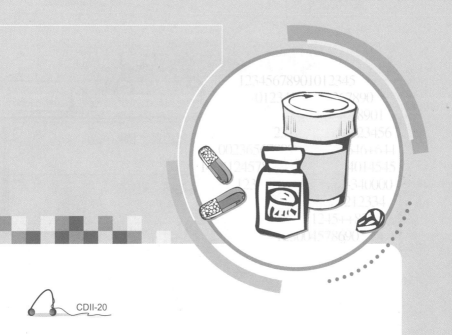

CDII-20

A diet filled with delicious whole foods is of course the preferred way to receive all of the important vitamins and minerals the body requires. However, in this day and age, there are many excuses as to why we don't eat the foods we should. If you choose to pop supplements, remember to always do your research. Supplements are drugs and need to be treated as such!

基本行話 The Lingo

CDII-21

❶ daily amount [ˈdelɪ əˈmaʊnt]	每日用量、攝取量 *n.*	
❷ vitamin [ˈvaɪtəmɪn]	維他命；維生素 *n.*	
❸ mineral [ˈmɪnərəl]	礦物質 *n.*	
❹ supplement [ˈsʌpləmənt]	補充；補給品 *n.*	
❺ multivitamin [ˌmʌltɪˈvaɪtəmɪn]	綜合維他命 *n.*	
❻ energy bar [ˈɛnədʒɪ ˌbɑr]	能量棒 *n.*	
❼ label [ˈlebl̩]	標籤 *n.*	
❽ meal replacement powder [ˈmil rɪˈplesmənt ˌpaʊdə]	代餐粉 *n.*	
❾ protein [ˈprotiɪn]	蛋白質 *n.*	
❿ herb [ɝb]	藥草 *n.*	

暖身練習 Word Workout

CDII-22

A:I feel like I don't receive the recommended **daily amount** of **vitamins** and **minerals**.
B:You could try taking a **supplement** such as a **multivitamin**.

A:我覺得好像沒有獲得每日建議的維生素及礦物質攝取量。
B:你可以試試吃補給品，比方綜合維他命。

A:I don't need food — I just chowed down on an **energy bar** before I went to work out.
B:Did you read the **label**? Some bars contain more fat and calories than you eat in a meal!

A:我不需要吃東西了——我運動前才吃了一條能量棒。
B:你有看食品標籤嗎？有些能量棒含的脂肪和熱量比你吃一餐還多呢！

A:**Meal replacement powders** seem to really help a lot of people.
B:Those powders are good for people who don't eat enough **protein** and want to lose body fat.

A:代餐粉似乎真的對很多人大有幫助。
B:那些餐粉適合蛋白質攝取不足和想降低體脂的人。

A:I try to use **herbs** when I cook.
B:That's great. Many herbs have disease-fighting nutrients.

A:我嘗試在烹飪的時候用些藥草。
B:那很好啊。很多藥草都有對抗疾病的營養成分。

 健美會話 1  Talk the Talk

 CDII-23

(Alan and Jerry are walking around town.)

Alan: I've got to go in this supplement shop. I need some **flaxseed oil** and a multi vitamin.

Jerry: Great. I want to buy some egg protein, the drink of champions.

Alan: Are you serious? Why **on earth** do you need **protein shakes**?

Jerry: Because protein gives the body **amino acids**, which are the **building blocks** for muscles. Since you started **bulking up**, I figured I should, too.

Alan: Jerry, you don't work out. You can't build muscle unless you work your muscles.

Jerry: You just don't want any competition. I **read up on** this stuff, man. I know what I am talking about.

Alan: OK, Mr. Know-It-All. How are you going to gain muscle without working out?

Jerry: I need to have a **high-protein**, **low-carb** diet.

Alan: Ha, ha, ha!

Jerry: What are you laughing at?

Alan: You are on a bodybuilder's diet without actually bodybuilding. **You are truly a piece of work**, Jerry.

（艾倫和傑瑞正在市區裡蹓躂）

艾倫：我得進這家賣營養補給品的商店。我需要一些亞麻子油和一罐綜合維他命。

傑瑞：太好了。我想買蛋蛋白，那種給冠軍喝的飲品。

艾倫：你說真的嗎？你究竟為什麼需要蛋白質飲品？

傑瑞：因為蛋白質能提供身體氨基酸，而氨基酸是肌肉的構成要素。既然你開始變壯了，我想我也應該要一樣。

艾倫：傑瑞，你又不運動。除非你鍛鍊你的肌肉，否則不可能強健肌肉的。

傑瑞：你就是不想比是吧。我可是特別研究過的喔，老兄。我知道自己在說什麼。

艾倫：好吧，「萬事通」先生。你要如何不運動就長肌肉呢？

傑瑞：我需要吃高蛋白、低碳水化合物的飲食。

艾倫：哈哈哈！

傑瑞：你笑什麼？

艾倫：你吃健美人士的飲食，但實際上卻沒有在健美。還真有你的啊，傑瑞。

Words & Phrases

1. flaxseed oil [ˈflæks͵sid ͵ɔɪl] n. 亞麻子油

2. on earth 究竟；到底

3. protein shake [ˈprotiɪn ͵ʃek] n. 高蛋質飲品

4. amino acid [əˈmino ˈæsɪd] n. 氨基酸

5. building block [ˈbɪldɪŋ ͵blɑk] n. 構成要素；建築的木材

6. bulk [bʌlk] up 脹大；壘起

7. read up on 鑽研；詳讀

8. high-protein [ˈhaɪˈprotiɪn] adj. 高蛋白的

9. low-carb [ˈloˈkɑrb] adj. 低碳水化合物的

10. You're truly a piece of work. 還真有你的。

健美會話2　Walk the Walk

CDII-24

(Alan explains some things to Jerry.)

Alan: Look, the phrase "no pain, no gain" truly **applies** here. If you keep **consuming** that much protein without working out, you'll end up with disease, not muscle.

Jerry: I looked this up on the Internet. It said I should have around one gram of protein per one pound of body weight.

Alan: That is for **strength trainers**. Too much protein can leave you **dehydrated**, give you **kidney stones** or cause **osteoporosis**.

Jerry: This **sucks**. The can I bought the powder in says I would build muscle, lose fat and get strong. I feel **ripped off**!

Alan: Well, you could start working out.

Jerry: Dude, I don't know what to do. Just the thought of **exerting** that much energy exhausts me.

(An attractive woman walks up to Alan.)

Woman: Hi. It looks like you work out. Here's my number – call me some time and we can work out together.

Jerry: Uh ... so when did you say you were going to the gym again?

(艾倫向傑瑞解釋一些事情)

艾倫：聽著，「吃得苦中苦，方為人上人」這句話在這裡挺適用的。如果你繼續吃那麼多的蛋白質卻不運動，最後只會生病，而不是長肌肉。

傑瑞：我有在網路上查過。上面說每一磅的體重應攝取大約一公克的蛋白質。

艾倫：那是肌力教練用的。蛋白質過多會讓你脫水，造成腎結石或導致骨質疏鬆。

傑瑞：真是討厭。我買的那罐蛋白質粉上面標示說，我會增長肌肉、減少脂肪，還會變強壯。我覺得被坑了！

艾倫：嗯，你可以開始運動啊。

傑瑞：老兄，我不知道該做什麼。光是想到要用那麼多力氣就讓我覺得好累。

(一位迷人的女士走向艾倫)

女士：嗨，你看起來有在運動健身。這是我的電話號碼——有空打電話給我，我們可以一起運動。

艾倫：呃……你說你什麼時候會再去健身房？

Words & Phrases

1. apply [ə`plaɪ] *v.* 適用；適合

2. consume [kən`sum] *v.* 吃；喝；消耗

3. strength trainer [`strɛŋθ ˏtrenɚ] *n.*
   肌力教練

4. dehydrated [di`haɪdretɪd] *adj.* 脫水的

5. kidney stone [`kɪdnɪ ˏston] *n.* 腎結石

6. osteoporosis [ˏɑstɪopə`rosɪs] *n.*
   骨質疏鬆（症）

7. suck [sʌk] *v.* 【口】令人討厭

8. rip off 敲竹槓

9. exert [ɪg`zɝt] *v.* 使力；運用
   （力氣、權力等）

活力金句 Q&A Pop-up Q&A

■ 也許你會想問⋯⋯

CDII-25

【營養補給品怎麼挑？】

你： How do I choose a **brand** of vitamin and mineral supplement?

我要如何選擇維他命和礦物質補給品的牌子呢？

專家： Look for **organic ingredients**. Check the **expiration date** and make sure the nutrients have been tested.

找有機成份的。檢查有效期限，並確定營養份經過測試。

【自由基有什麼問題？】

你： What are **free radicals**?

什麼叫自由基？

專家： Free radicals can **damage cells** and **accelerate cancer**. They come from **toxins** such as cigarettes and foods that contain **chemicals**.

自由基會破壞細胞，促發癌症。它們來自一些毒素，比如香煙和含有化學物質的食物。

【什麼是抗氧化？】

你： What are **antioxidants**?

什麼叫抗氧化劑？

專家： Antioxidants are nutrients that slow down damage caused by free radicals.

抗氧化劑是可以減低由自由基所引起的傷害的營養素。

130

■ 也許你會想說……

【來不及吃東西！】

你： Sometimes I am too rushed after working out to have time to eat.
有時在運動之後，我會因為太趕而沒有時間吃東西。

專家： Put some energy-giving foods in your bag for after your workout.
在你的袋子裡放一些補充體力的食物，好在運動後吃。

【身為懶骨頭……】

你： I always feel sluggish! I hate it but I don't want to work out.
我老是覺得懶洋洋的！我討厭這樣，但我就是不想運動。

專家： Try eating healthier food and **fit in** a walk a few times a week.
試著吃比較健康的食物，一星期騰出一些時間散步幾次。

 Words & Phrases

1. brand [brænd] *n.* 廠牌；品牌

2. organic [ɔr`gænɪk] *adj.* 有機的

3. ingredient [ɪn`gridɪənt] *n.* 成份；原料

4. expiration date [.ɛkspə`reʃən .det] *n.* 有效期限

5. free radical [`fri `rædɪkl] *n.* 自由基

6. damage [`dæmɪdʒ] *v.* 傷害；破壞

7. cell [sɛl] *n.* 細胞

8. accelerate [æk`sɛlə.ret] *v.* 促進；加速

9. cancer [`kænsɚ] *n.* 癌症

10. toxin [`tɑksɪn] *n.* 毒素

11. chemical [`kɛmɪkl] *n.* 化學物質

12. antioxidant [.æntaɪ`ɑksɪdənt] *n.* 抗氧化劑

13. fit in 騰出時間（做某事）；（使）符合；適應

健美加油站 Q A Inspiration Lounge

■ 維他命何處有？ Where You Get Vitamins

　　如果你的飲食無法提供足夠的營養，不妨補充維他命，讓身體能正常快樂地運作！

- 維他命 A

　　功用：對於維持視力（vision）、健康的皮膚及組織（tissue）都有功效，是一種抗氧化劑（antioxidant）。

　　來源：鮮橘色的水果及蔬菜，如芒果、甜瓜、杏桃（apricot）、木瓜、橘子、胡蘿蔔和番茄等。另外，蛋、肝臟（liver）和乳製品的含量都很高。

- 維他命 B

　　功用：指維他命 B 群（vitamin B complex），包括維他命 B1、B2、B3、B5、B6 和 B12，協助身體各種機能，例如腦部功能、皮膚、頭髮生長和修護，以及神經（nerve）功能。維他命 B 還有助於將蛋白質、脂肪和碳水化合物轉換成能量。

　　來源：草莓、水田芥（watercress）、青椒、番茄、酪梨（avocado）、香蕉、瘦肉、全穀類、堅果類和種籽類。

- 維他命 C

　　功用：促進健康的結締組織（connective tissue）生長，預防感染（infection），增強抵抗力。

　　來源：這種強效的抗氧化劑可從柑橘類水果中攝取。多吃鳳梨、芒果、木瓜、奇異果、甜瓜、番茄和青椒。

- 維他命 E

　　功用：為另一種對抗自由基的強力抗氧化劑，對防止皮膚老化（aging）很有效，同時有助於穩定情緒。

　　來源：全穀麵包、小麥胚芽、深綠色蔬菜、種籽類和堅果類，例如芝麻、花生、南瓜子、杏仁（almond）、核桃（walnut）、腰果（cashew）、榛果（hazelnut）。

- 維他命 K

　　功用：為幫助身體製造血液凝固（blood clotting）所需之蛋白質的基本物質，
　　　　　亦能增加骨骼的礦物質含量及硬度。

　　來源：深綠色蔬菜，尤其是花椰菜、萵苣、波菜和水田芹。

■ 礦物質為何很重要？ Why Are Minerals So Special?

　　礦物質是我們身體的好夥伴。礦物質能讓我們的骨骼、細胞和組織維持健
康。人體所需最重要的礦物質為鈣 (calcium)、鐵 (iron) 和鋅 (zinc)。有些礦物質
屬微量礦物質 (trance minerals)，人體所需的量很少，這包括了鋅、硒 (seleni-
um)、鐵、碘 (iodine) 和鉻 (chromium)。需要劑量較多的有鈣、磷 (phosphorus)
和鎂 (magnesium)。

■ 越多不見得越好 More Is Not Always Better!

　　每個人都應該從他們的食物中攝取所需的維他命，在某些特殊情況下才會需
要營養補充品，例如受訓中的運動員、某些疾病的患者和素食者。但不管怎麼
樣，如果你有使用這些補充品，一定要依照建議的劑量（dosage）服用。「補
充越多的維他命和礦物質能讓身體越健康、越強壯」，這是無稽之談（myth）。
事實上，如果你體內的維他命和礦物質過多，一部份會囤積在你的體脂肪內，
最後成為毒素。一般來說，隨一天的正餐吃適量的營養補充品是安全的。但是
要記住一點，很多人花了太多錢在他們根本不需要的營養補充品上。為了幫自
己省錢，你應該找個營養師談談，以確定你是否需要額外補充維他命和礦物
質。

Real champions believe in themselves
　　　　　　　even when no one else will!
　　　　　　　　　　　　　— Anonymous

真正的贏家相信自己，縱使沒有人相信他們！
　　　　　　　　　　　　　——佚名

Chapter 11

Organic Food
天然純淨的有機食品

「有機」這個字指的是食品的生產製造方法。如果食品被標示為有機產品，就表示牲畜是在健康、天然的環境下飼養長大，或表示水果、蔬菜和穀物在栽種時未使用化學肥料。以傳統方式栽培的食物會留下環境遭破壞的痕跡，因為它們會污染土壤和水質。化肥或許有利於增加農民的收入，但也影響了消費者的健康，帶來疾病，而且栽種出來的食物也比較不營養。許多人已經轉而選擇有機食品，因為它們更美味、健康，而且比較不會污染環境。

CDII-26

The word "organic" refers to the way foods are produced. If a food is labeled organic, it means that animals are raised in healthy, natural conditions and fruits, vegetables and grains are grown without the use of chemicals. Conventionally grown foods leave behind a trail of environmental damage as they pollute the soil and water. Chemicals may benefit the farmer's paycheck, but they leave consumers with health complaints and less nutritious food. Many people have turned to organic foods because they are tastier, healthier and more environmentally friendly.

Healthy Living

CDII-27

❶ conventionally [kən`vɛnʃən]ɪ]	傳統地；因襲地 *adv.*
❷ organic [ɔr`gænɪk]	有機的 / 有機物 *adj./n.*
❸ inject [ɪn`jɛkt]	注射 *v.*
❹ hormone [`hɔrmon]	賀爾蒙 *n.*
❺ antibiotics [ˌæntɪbaɪ`ɑtɪks]	抗生素 *n.*
❻ overuse [`ovɚ`juz]	過度使用；濫用 *n.*
❼ resistant [rɪ`zɪstənt]	對……有抵抗力的 *adj.*
❽ compost [`kɑmpost]	堆肥 *n.*
❾ fertilizer [`fɚtl̩ˌaɪzɚ]	肥料 *n.*
❿ chemical [`kɛmɪkl̩]	化學的；化學物質 *adj./n.*

暖身練習 Word Workout

CDII-28

A: It is cheaper to produce and buy **conventionally**-grown foods.
B: **Organic** farming is more costly. But it won't damage the environment that much.

A: 生產和購買傳統栽培的食物比較便宜。
B: 有機農業成本比較高，但是對環境的傷害沒那麼大。

A: How can chickens grow naturally in such cramped henhouses?
B: That's why farmers have to **inject hormones** to stimulate their muscle mass.

A: 雞在那麼狹窄的雞舍怎麼自然生長呢？
B: 這就是為什麼農人必須注射賀爾蒙來促進牠們肌肉量的增長。

A: Why is the use of **antibiotics** an issue?
B: **Overuse** of antibiotics makes the animals **resistant** to them and encourages disease.

A: 為什麼使用抗生素會是個問題呢？
B: 過度使用抗生素會讓牲畜產生抗藥性，還會促發疾病。

A: My grandparents used **compost** as an organic **fertilizer**.
B: Agriculture has changed so much. **Chemicals** are widely used nowadays.

A: 我的祖父母用堆肥來作有機肥料。
B: 農業改變了很多。現在化學用品的使用很廣泛。

 健美會話 1 Talk the Talk

 CDII-29

(Diane is teaching Jerry how to choose healthy foods .)

Diane: You have done really well making changes in your diet.

Jerry: Thanks. Since you and Alan have helped me with my diet, I have lost some weight and I feel healthier.

Diane: That is so great to hear! Let's go to an organic store today and you can fill up your fridge with **yummy toxin-free** foods.

Jerry: Diane, I'm not rich. Buying organic costs too much money.

Diane: You will end up spending even more money on the doctor. He'll have to fix all the problems you'll get from eating conventionally-grown food.

Jerry: Ha ha. That's not true. Is it?

Diane: Sure. Chemicals used on fruits and vegetables can cause us to have **memory loss**, **vision** problems, **anxiety**, **digestion** problems and even depression.

Jerry: That's great!

Diane: What do you mean that's great?!

Jerry: Well, I can use the food I eat as an excuse for forgetting my mom's birthday!

（黛安在教傑瑞如何選擇健康食品）

黛安：你在改變飲食方面做得非常好呢。

傑瑞：謝啦。自從你和艾倫幫我調整飲食以來，我已經減了一些體重，
　　　而且覺得比較健康了。

黛安：聽起來真是太棒了！咱們今天去有機食品店，你可以把冰箱塞滿
　　　好吃又無毒的食物。

傑瑞：黛安，我並不富有。買有機食品太花錢了。

黛安：那你最後會落得花更多錢看醫生。他得幫你解決所有你因為吃傳
　　　統栽培食物所引起的疑難雜症。

傑瑞：哈哈，沒那回事啦。會這樣嗎？

黛安：當然。水果蔬菜上用的化學藥品會導致失憶、視力問題、焦慮、
　　　消化不良，甚至憂鬱。

傑瑞：那真是太好了！

黛安：你說太好了是什麼意思？！

傑瑞：嗯，我可以把我吃的食物當作忘記我媽生日的藉口了！

 Words & Phrases

1. yummy [ˈjʌmɪ] *adj.* 好吃的；可口的

2. toxin-free [ˈtɔksɪnˋfri] *adj.* 無毒的

3. memory loss [ˈmɛmərɪ ˌlɔs] *n.* 失憶

4. vision [ˈvɪʒən] *n.* 視力

5. anxiety [æŋˋzaɪətɪ] *n.* 焦慮

6. digestion [daɪˋdʒɛstʃən] *n.* 消化

7. depression [dɪˋprɛʃən] *n.* 沮喪；憂鬱

健美會話2　Walk the Walk

CDII-30

(At an organic store)

Jerry:　Health risk or not, I can't afford to pay these prices.

Diane: Well, some products contain more chemicals than others. Just buy organic versions of those.

Jerry:　OK, that sounds good. Where do we start?

Diane: Milk.

Jerry:　No way, milk can't be bad for you. It's so **wholesome**!

Diane: That is what **dairy** companies want you to think. Cows are **frequently** injected with hormones. It helps them produce more milk.

Jerry:　That doesn't sound so bad.

Diane: Well, it wouldn't be if the **milk pumps** attached to their **udders** didn't cause disease and skin **infections**.

Jerry:　The poor cows!

Diane: That's not all. The hormone used on cows called rBGH has not been fully tested to find out how it **affects** humans. Links have been made to **tumor** growth as well as **prostate** and breast cancer.

Jerry:　Diane, **do me a favor** and hand me a **carton** of that organic milk, please.

（在有機食品專賣店）

傑瑞：不管會不會造成健康的風險，我付不起這些價錢。

黛安：嗯，有些產品比起其他含更多的化學物質。你只要買那些有機製造的就好了。

傑瑞：好，聽起來不錯。我們從何開始？

黛安：牛奶。

傑瑞：不會吧，牛奶怎麼可能會對人體有壞處。牛奶那麼有益健康！

黛安：乳品公司就是希望你這麼想。乳牛經常被注射賀爾蒙。那有助牠們製造更多牛奶。

傑瑞：聽起來沒那麼糟啊。

黛安：嗯，如果附在牛乳頭上的擠乳機不引發疾病和皮膚感染就不會那麼糟了。

傑瑞：可憐的乳牛！

黛安：還不止呢。施打在牛隻身上的賀爾蒙叫做「基因重組牛隻生長激素」，至今還沒完全測試出會對人類產生什麼影響。但目前已知那和腫瘤的生成以及攝護腺癌和乳癌都有關。

傑瑞：黛安，幫我一個忙，請把那一盒有機牛奶拿給我。

 Words & Phrases

1. wholesome [ˋholsəm] *adj.*
   合乎衛生的；有益健康的

2. dairy [ˋdɛrɪ] *adj.* 酪農的

3. frequently [ˋfrikwəntlɪ] *adv.* 頻繁地

4. milk pump [ˋmɪlk ˏpʌmp] *n.* 擠乳器

5. udder [ˋʌdə] *n.* 牛乳頭

6. infection [ɪnˋfɛkʃən] *n.* 傳染（病）

7. affect [əˋfɛkt] *v.* 影響

8. tumor [ˋtjumə] *n.* 腫瘤

9. prostate [ˋprɑstet] *n.* 攝護腺

10. do sb. a favor 幫某人一個忙

11. carton [ˋkɑrtṇ] *n.* 紙盒容器

活力金句 Ｑ Ａ Pop-up Q&A

■ 也許你會想問······

【有機和放養是什麼？】

你： What is the difference between organic and free range?
　　有機飼養和自由放養有什麼差別？

專家： Free range does not **guarantee** the animals eat organic. But both **receive** no hormone **injections** and almost never need antibiotics.
　　自由放養並不保證牲畜吃的是有機飼料。但兩者都沒有接受賀爾蒙注射，也幾乎不需要抗生素。

【傳統和有機有啥不同？】

你： Other than the use of chemicals, how else do conventionally-grown and organically-grown foods differ?
　　除了使用化學肥料，傳統栽陪和有機栽培的食品有何不同？

專家： Organically-grown foods are picked in season, leading to more nutrition and **flavor**. Conventionally-grown foods are **coated** with a **preservative**, giving the food an unnaturally long **life span**.
　　有機栽培的食品是季節採收，能有更多營養及美味。傳統栽培的食品則會上防腐劑，讓食物有不自然的長久保存期。

【殺蟲劑有多毒？】

你： Why are **pesticides** so bad? 為什麼殺蟲劑那麼糟糕？

專家： According to the WHO, more than three million people worldwide become sick and 220,000 die from pesticides every year.
　　根據世界衛生組織的資料，每年全世界有三百多萬人因為殺蟲劑致病、二十二萬人喪命。

■ 也許你會想說……

【買東西一定要多問】

朋友： I always ask many questions when I go to that store. People must think I am stupid.

我去那家店時總是問很多問題。那裡的人一定覺得我很笨。

你： You just want to know more about the things they sell. They're glad to help!

你只是想多了解他們販售的產品。他們很樂意協助的！

【看起來水噹噹】

你： Wow! I have really noticed a change in your skin lately. You look great!

哇！我最近真的注意到了你膚質的改善。你看起來很棒喔！

朋友： Thank you. It must be the organic strawberries I've been having for breakfast!

謝謝你。一定是因為我早餐吃的有機草莓的關係！

Words & Phrases

1. guarantee [ˌgærənˋti] v. 保證

2. receive [rɪˋsiv] v. 接受

3. injection [ɪnˋjɛkʃən] n. 注射

4. flavor [ˋflevə] n. 味道；風味

5. coat [kot] v. 裹；覆

6. preservative [prɪˋzɝvətɪv] n. 防腐劑

7. life span [ˋlaɪf ˌspæn] n. 生命週期

8. pesticide [ˋpɛstɪˌsaɪd] n. 殺蟲劑

健美加油站 Inspiration Lounge

要適應純有機的生活方式可能相當不容易。這裡提供幾種過有機生活的簡單方法。

▨ 人如其食 You Are What You Eat

如果買有機食品會讓你破產，那就只在你的購物清單中加幾樣有機物品。蘋果、蘋果汁、紅蘿蔔、西洋梨、草莓、牛肉、鮭魚（salmon）、牛奶等等，這些食物很有營養，但也容易含有高量化學物質，所以這些食物盡量買有機栽培或飼養的。

▨ 自己種香料 Grow Your Own Herbs

種香料不需要很大的空間，而且用新鮮香料烹調的好處不勝枚舉。自己種的香料不僅能提升食物的美味，你也知道它們是從哪來的，而且又比到超市買要便宜。如果你有個窗台或陽台，你就可以擁有個人的香料園，採收自己栽培的成果。簡單容易栽種的香料包括：薄荷 (mint)、奧勒岡 (oregano)、羅勒 (basil)、西洋芹 (parsley)、鼠尾草 (sage)、薰衣草 (lavender)、香蜂草 (lemon balm)。

▨ 食物以外的問題 Not Just Food

你知道用在棉花 (cotton) 上的幾種化學藥劑是農業用藥中毒性最強的嗎？光是在美國，每一年就用掉六十萬噸的各種化學藥物來種植棉花。棉花農面臨各種不同的壓力，迫使他們必須用具有破壞性的種植方法。對廉價棉花的大量需求，加上缺乏資金補助有機農民，使自然種植難以推行。

▨ 我能做什麼？ What Can I Do?

你可以選購有機栽培的棉花來支持自然農業，以創造出市場需求。你也可以考慮多用麻 (hemp) 製品。麻和棉一樣用途廣泛，抗蟲性卻較強，需要的水分較少，而且一英畝的麻所生產的可用材料和四英畝的棉一樣多。